CHANCES

By Michael Covington

Triple Crown Publications
PO Box 6888
Columbus, Ohio 43205
www.TripleCrownPublications.com

Library of Congress Control Number: 2006902054
ISBN: 0-9767894-7-7
ISBN 13: 978-0-9767894-7-5
Cover Design/Graphics: www.MarionDesigns.com
Author: Michael Covington
Typesetting: Holscher Type and Design
Associate Editors: Cynthia Parker, Rhonda Crowder
Editorial Assistant: Elizabeth Zaleski
Editor-in-Chief: Mia McPherson
Consulting: Vickie M. Stringer

First Trade Paperback Edition Printing March 2007

10 9 8 7 6 5 4 3 2 1

Printed in the United States of America

Acknowledgements

First, I must thank God for blessing me and guiding me through the many storms of life.

To my mother, Doris Covington, thanks for the love and support that you have given me my entire life. There are no words that righteously express what you mean to me. I LOVE YOU!!!!!!

To my kids: Antwain Hobbs, Justin Jordan, Asia and Mikia Covington, I know the time we lost can never be replaced, yet I hope that it's not too late to recapture the bond that ignorance and incarceration has denied me, and in return, denied you. The tragedies of life that don't destroy us make us stronger. Without you all I am nothing!!!!!

Not everyone's as fortunate to have the family support that I have and I'm definitely thankful for that. So, here's to the FAM: Anwar, (brother) you my nigga for real! Remember what we talked about? Blaze two, one for me one for you. Levon, (brother) picture us rollin'. Cynthia, (sister) no matter how mad I get I still love

you, girl. To Walter, Sarah, Bell, Issac, Barbara, Gabe, Shirley, Bazell, Greta, Beck, NeNe, I love y'all just the same. And to all I didn't have the room to mention, I got you on the next one, no doubt.

Special thanks to: Channon Lynette Jordan, you are the greatest!! Thanks for everything you have done for me and my sons. Much love, Bookie; Oletha Miller, the best god-sister in the world. I KNOW Heaven must be missin' an angel. Thanks babygirl!! Rhonda Snell, I don't know what I did to deserve you, but you are simply incredible. Without you none of this would have been possible. A million and one thanks to you!! Dr. Mutulu Shakur, my comrade, mentor and friend. You've shown me the true meaning of brotherhood. Together we struggle, resiliently we overcome. See you in the whirlwind!! Tony Walker, thanks for the long grueling hours that you spent typing and typing and retyping *Chances*. Do I owe you something? (smile) John "Strap" Harris, thanks for the bars to *Chances*. Remember, we locked in nigga! I don't think they ready for what we fixin' to do, feel me? Jondhi "Jay" Harrell, thanks for all your artistic work, support and encouragement. Navaro (Latif) stay strong, baby boy. The struggle don't stop!!!!

Dr. Umoja Akinyele, Dr. Shirlene Holmes, Dr. Nandi Crosby, GSU Blk. Studies Dept., N"Cobra ATL, WFRG 89.3 (Iras & Malik) Joycelyn Wilson, Olimatta Taal, Mawi, Kiara, Adrian and the crew, thanks for all the times y'all gave us a platform to express our opinions,

talents and concerns. How can I ever forget that!! Thanks Mr. R. Streeter (you did the best you could)!

To that Chi-Town click ... Anthony White, Michael Jackson, Anthony Davis, Bezo, Chris, Fast Eddie, Mo, Silk, Bobby, E. Scott, JC, OG Binion. One Love, homies!!!!!!!

Please don't let me forget these special people ... DeMarcus Osborne (you ready to ride?); Penelithea "P'Nut" Devaughn (stay in those books, everything else will come naturally); Dorian Allen (college is to get an education, remember?); Jillian Jordan (Uncle Mike got your back!); Roshann Whirfield (Damn! We finally met!); T. Plair, holla at cha boy! Swain, Pate, Black, Furley, it's my time to shine, fo sho!!!! Valencia Johnson, don't make me tell the whole world (smile); Sydney Rambert Jr., get at me!

And last but not least, a big big big shout out goes to Vickie Stringer, Triple Crown Publications and staff (Mia, Tammy, Amanda, my editor Cynthia Parker and crew) for believing in a playa. Thanks!!!!

Haterz ... keep hatin'. One.

Triple Crown Publications presents . . .

Dedication

To my grandmother, Emma Ephraim.
Rest in Peace.

Triple Crown Publications presents . . .

ONE

As the sunshine seeped through the blinds, casting a ray of light across his face, DeAndre awakened startled. Hastily, he sat up in the bed, thinking that he had overslept. "One more muthafuckin' time," he whispered as he stretched, getting out of bed.

It was moments before he realized he was no longer a federal prisoner, no longer had to be up by sunrise to report to work. It was the day he'd been waiting on for six years, although it took him a minute to grasp this realization.

The thought of his partnas left behind caused his brow to furrow and his happiness to briefly fade because he knew they were still trapped inside of that concrete jungle, trying to survive in what was to be

their home for the rest of their lives. He left J-Boogie, Dollar and Killa, all with Buck Rogers time, promising to hold them down.

He checked his wrist for the time then realized he had given his watch away, wanting nothing to remind him of where he had been. Everything about his past, from the death of his parents to his incarceration, haunted him daily.

A knock, followed by a voice at the door, snapped him out of his early morning daydream.

"Yeah, what's up, Dee?"

"Dre, you trying to eat breakfast or what?" asked Deidre, his sister.

Dee Dee, as most of her closest friends called her, couldn't boil water without burning the pot. Her cooking skills had been the source of some of DeAndre's funniest jokes ever since they were little. It pissed her off though.

Standing up to find a pair of sweats, Dre noticed a familiar sensation in between his legs. Looking down, a morning erection greeted him. *I gotta get this taken care of,* he thought. Deidre knocked again as he put on his jogging pants.

"Dre...Dre! You gon' eat or not?"

"I don't know, baby girl. It would be a shame to have escaped all the shit I been through, then come home and die from food poisoning my first day out."

She burst into the room with a grin on her face.

"Oh, so you got jokes this morning, huh? Boy, don't make me punch you."

Dre fell back on the bed, laughing at her. She stood with her hands on her hips as if she had an attitude. He still hadn't gotten over how grown up and fine his little sister had become.

"Damn, girl! Don't be busting up in my room like dat. What if you had come in and found one of your lil' girlfriends in the buck, serving a nigga? Then your mouth would be all twisted up."

"Man, please! I don't know why these chicks acting like you the best thing since tampons. You ain't really all that, partna!"

"You can't stand when one of your friends get caught up in the midst of this thug lovin'. You know ya'll be all up on a thorough nigga. Don't hate...appreciate."

The penitentiary had preserved him, and at twenty-eight years old, he was in the best shape of his life. Standing six feet even, two hundred fifteen pounds, Dre should've been on somebody's football team. Instead, he was a hustler. The streets were his gridiron and his goal was to get rich.

"You are so shady, Dre," Deidre said, shaking her head at his last comment. "Come on and eat before your food gets cold." She turned and left the room.

Deidre was a year younger than Dre, although they were always mistaken for twins. She was a direct con-

trast to his rough and rugged looks. At five-foot-six, she was a player's dream come true. Squares too, but they never stood a chance because she was infatuated with expensive things, items only the wealthy could afford. Every man she ever had was in the game. The streets raised her, and it was hard to do something different when that was the only life she knew.

Rich, a major playa, was filthy rich, and he gave his money to her recklessly. He kept her laced with the newest clothes, vehicles and jewelry, and it was his generosity that enabled her to purchase a nice home in Calumet City, a southern suburb of Chicago. Yet, his support wasn't without consequence. She kept this information from her brother though. He didn't need to know all her business. The only person she confided in was her best friend, Mya. She was the only one who knew the extent of Dee Dee and Rich's relationship and the abuse she suffered at his hands.

At the dining room table, Dre waited as he watched Dee Dee move throughout the kitchen. She soon appeared, bringing out two plates filled with food. He was curious about her life since he had been gone.

"Dee, what's been going on with you?" he asked as he shoveled a forkful of eggs in his mouth.

"Same shit, different day. Tired of working my ass off for someone else. I'm ready to get my own."

"I'm feeling that. You know I'm getting ready to make a move, and when I do, I got you." Remembering

his arrival yesterday, he was impressed with how his little sister was living. "You sitting on some stacks, huh?" he asked, admiring the intricate artwork and imported furniture.

"I'm cool...I mean I'm sittin' on a lil' something but it takes more money than I expected to keep up this place, especially when you're still trying to live...you know." Dee Dee spoke, trying her best seem to preoccupied.

Dre couldn't quite put his hands on the look he saw in her eyes, like she was holding something back.

"Who is this dude, Rich, I keep hearing so much about? I know he breaking bread, or are you giving up the goodies for free?"

"First of all that's none of yo' business." Dee Dee rolled her eyes up to the ceiling. "And secondly he all right. He cool, I guess. I ain't tryin' to make no family wit that nigga if that's what you think. I'm just simply playin' the relationship for what it's worth."

"Well, I ain't got no beef with that as long as he treating you right. You know some niggas get controlling once they start dropping them ends." After biting into a biscuit and washing it down with some orange juice, he asked, "He don't be hitting on you, do he?"

Dee Dee lowered the fork in her hand and peered at him. *Why this nigga have to go there*, she thought. She was never good at hiding things from Dre. Yet, she knew she could never tell him the truth. Rich had been slapping her around a lot lately, but hell, Dre didn't have to know that. Some things were just better left unsaid.

"Guess what? I got something in the garage for you," Dee Dee said, changing the subject.

"What is it?"

"Go see for yourself. The safe should be open," she said with a smirk on her face, piquing Dre's curiosity.

Like a kid at Christmas, Dre abandoned the rest of his almost-finished breakfast to see what his sister had waiting for him.

Later that afternoon, Dre found himself leaning against the hood of his Ford Mustang. The ten grand his sister gave him lay spread out over the hood. No matter how much he insisted, she wouldn't take the money back. She said she was good, remembering when he used to be the one giving. He smiled.

"Damn! Seems like the shoe is on the other foot now." He put the money away and grabbed a bucket and towels, deciding to clean his ride.

As he vacuumed out the inside of the car, he came across a photo of himself and his ex-girlfriend Monica. They were on the lakefront a few days before he got sentenced. In a trance, he stared at her, looking for a sign of the imminent desertion he faced when he needed her the most.

After he was locked up, their relationship went spiraling downhill. He was stressed out by having to do

some time and she couldn't fathom being alone for the next ten years. After his first year down, all contact ceased. Dre was crushed, but he had to face the fact that she had shitted on him and moved on. That was five years ago. He figured he was long over her, but looking at her picture, he realized that wasn't the case. Thinking back on his time in the penitentiary and the chances he took to provide her with material things, he ripped the photo to shreds. "All the bricks I threw for that bitch!" he exclaimed.

He promised to never let another woman's absence affect him the way Monica's did. It never dawned on him that the only thing he ever gave her was money, heartache and pain because he was so much into his feelings and pissed off. On Monica's end the money never meant a thing. It was his love, time and affection that she wanted the most. Once she was alone with time to think, the three easily outweighed the one.

Dre washed his car as well as Dee Dee's. As he was sitting in the back yard smoking a blunt, his cell phone rang.

Looking at the caller ID, it was his boy Eric. "What's up, playa?"

"Hey, stop through a little later on. I need to holla at you about something important."

Dre took a long drag from the blunt. "Aight. Peace."

"Peace."

Eric and Dre knew each other before they became cellmates in the joint, but that's where they bonded like brothers. Although Eric had gotten out two years prior, they remained tight. He assured Dre that everything would be all right once he returned home.

After finishing his blunt, Dre went inside the house. He took a shower and dressed in one of the hook ups Dee Dee bought him then rolled out.

As he cruised the South Holland neighborhood looking for Eric's spot, he admired all the fabulous cribs. *Damn, E doin' his thing! I wonder how long it will be before I can get a joint like this*, he thought to himself. He knew his partna was pushing major weight and had just purchased the house, but he never imagined it to be as large of an estate as the ones he saw.

It took him twenty minutes before he found the house, nestled back off the road in a cul-de-sac. He noticed the strategically placed security lights and cameras throughout the exterior of the expansive property as he entered the driveway. He brought his out-of-place Mustang to rest behind a brand new, powder blue 745 BMW. The personalized plates read "E-Mo," a nickname he and Eric shared with each other. It was good to think of E-Mo and D-Mo being back together. An impressed chuckle escaped his lips.

My man is on some serious shit, he thought to himself as he climbed the stairs. He listened to the elaborate sounds of the doorbell while he took in his surround-

ings. Startled by a female scream, Dre turned back to the door. Trina, Eric's girl, ran into his arms.

"Hey, Dre! Welcome home!" Trina hugged him tightly, pressing her entire body against his.

He was caught off-guard as he enjoyed the wonderful feeling of having a woman in his arms again. He and Trina had known each other forever. He was the reason she and Eric were together. Although there was a slight attraction between the two, they never acted upon it. Now, as she was up in his arms, it was obvious nothing had changed. Knowing his mind had slipped into forbidden territory, he released her, stepping back onto safe grounds. He shook his head and both of them understood.

"Where's my man?"

"He's out on the patio waiting for you." She smiled as she grabbed him by the hand, leading him into the house.

It was useless for him to try to avoid watching her ass as it bounced from side to side. The sheer black veil around her waist did little to hide the yellow material of her thong as it disappeared between the crack of her behind.

The snow white carpet, crystal chandeliers and marble trimmings seemed endless as they traveled through the house. Eric entered through another door as they stepped into the den. Trina retreated in a different direction.

At the sight of Dre, he embraced him in a one-arm hug, the traditional bond of a black man.

"Man, I never thought this day would come. It's good to see you, and it's damn good to be free, nigga," Dre said, returning his partna's embrace.

Trina reappeared with drinks for both of them. She stood in front of Eric and wrapped her arms around him, kissing him on the lips. Before she left the room, she turned toward Dre. "Ain't he looking good, Eric? I'm glad you're home, Dre."

Dre was somewhat uncomfortable with her comment, but it didn't seem to faze his partna. Without a second thought, he beckoned for Dre to follow him.

They walked toward the window and E hit the switch that retracted the blinds. Dre's eyes opened in disbelief as he observed the multitude of bikini-clad women jumping around, welcoming him home. A few select guys stood off to the side with bottles of Moët held high in the air. A sign saying, "WELCOME HOME DRE, WE MISSED YOU" stretched the length of the Olympic-sized pool.

"You are out cold with your shit," Dre said as a smile spread across his face.

"So are you," a voice from behind him replied, causing him to turn around. "Well… are you gonna just stand there or are you gonna come give me a hug?" asked a sexy, mocha-chocolate skinned sister.

Dre hesitated before speaking her name, not want-

ing to get it wrong. His surprise was evident. "Ebony? Man, this shit is getting better by the second." He approached her with his arms extended.

Ebony stood about five-foot-five, one hundred twenty pounds with a small waist and wide hips. But it was her hazel eyes that always drove him wild. She was a flight attendant from Southern Illinois that he had met while flying home from Jamaica one summer. She was also the one who introduced him to the Mile High Club. Whenever she flew into O'Hare Airport, they would get together, or when time permitted since he always stayed on the grind, hustling. They never had the chance to spend as much time as either of them desired. Yet, they remained intimate friends, even with Monica in the picture. Even after not seeing her for six years, their attraction to each other was still vibrant. They embraced, and he lifted her off the ground to spin her around. He was truly glad to see her again.

"Baby girl, this has *got* to be the best welcome home surprise of them all! How did you find out about the party?" he asked, placing her back on her feet.

Ebony rubbed her hands on his chest, feeling his sculptured muscles. "I ran into Eric last week when I was flying in from Kansas City. We both thought we knew each other and started talking. Once we figured it out, he told me that you were coming home and he was giving you a party. So…I'm here." She smiled her million-dollar smile and pulled him close, wanting to feel his body next to hers. She looked up and sighed. "That explains why I could never get in touch with you. Dre, you know you were dead wrong for not staying in touch with me." She looked away as she pouted.

Dre and Ebony's relationship was built on respect and mutual understanding. They were from different walks of life yet comfortable in each other's worlds. He slid his hands down her back and found a resting place on her ass. "I'm here now, so what's up?" he responded as he looked into her eyes.

"You know what, we can talk about that later," she said with a sly smile that ran across her lips. "I would hate for you to miss your own party because I kidnapped you." She reached her right hand down and felt his hard dick through his pants then raised an eyebrow. "You know I'm trying to get with you as soon as possible, but I'm not going no where, ever again. So, enjoy yourself because the night belongs to us. Come on, you need to change."

In the guest room, Ebony sat on the bed and handed Dre a pair of swim trunks. She crossed her legs, lay back and rested on her elbows. It was evident that she intended to watch as he undressed. He stepped out of his pants, and she licked her lips. Her eyes never left his crotch area. Her breath got caught in her throat as he pulled his boxers down, revealing a part of him she wanted so badly.

He looked at her unashamed. "Are you enjoying

yourself?"

"Not as much as I would be if you were a little closer."

He walked over to where she sat. "Well, you know I charge a fee for private shows."

"I'm willing to pay...whatever...to have some of this," she said, reaching out to touch his dick. She looked into his eyes as she took him in her mouth.

Dre ran his hands through her hair, enjoying his first shot of head since being home. The erotic sounds that escaped from her mouth heightened his arousal. She seemed to be enjoying herself just as much as he was, if that was possible. Sensing he was on the verge of cumming, she grabbed him by the ass and pulled him deeper into her mouth. She almost gagged as the first shots of cum hit the back of her throat. She continued, making sure that he was completely drained before she went into the bathroom with her toothbrush and towel.

"Ebony, what's up? You know I'm trying to hit that!" Dre hollered behind her.

She came back to the door and smiled at him seductively as she took off her clothes to change into her swimsuit. She motioned her finger for him to come closer. Dre enjoyed the up-close and personal show and couldn't wait to get a sneak peek at what was inside. Once she was completely naked, she turned her back to him as she pretended to pick something up off the floor. The sight of her sex, from behind, excited him even more. Stroking himself, he walked inside the bathroom. She spread her legs as she bent over the toilet, resting her elbows on the top. He slid his dick into her dripping pussy.

"Home sweet home," she purred as they found a rhythm.

"And I ain't goin' nowhere," he said as he started to pound away inside of her. The sounds of sex were music to his ears as she moaned, he grunted and the mixture of their most intimate parts met each other. That was a song he had not heard in years. Dre grabbed Ebony's ass and spread her cheeks, enjoying the sight of his dick going in and out of her slippery pussy. She shivered and juice ran down her long sexy legs. On the verge of cumming again, he increased his speed, and she put her hands in between her legs to massage her clit. She gave him her fingers to lick as he exploded inside of her succulent pussy, deeply coating it with his semen.

"Girl, your pussy is better than I remembered," he said, trying to catch his breath.

"Your stroke got a little deeper, big boy," she said, admiring the tool that just gave her pleasure. "You know what, we need to get cleaned up and go downstairs to the party. They gon' really think I kidnapped your ass." Sexually satisfied, they laughed, cleaned their bodies and joined the party, which was already jumping with everyone having a good time.

Dee Dee had a lot of her friends there, a few Dre

knew and some he had never seen before. With Ebony by his side, he mingled with everyone. The shouts of laughter and music could be heard for blocks. It wasn't long before the blunts and drinks took effect and everyone was on the lawn stepping, a dance similar to the two-step that originated in Chicago.

Time passed quickly and as evening neared, the party somewhat thinned out. Those who hung around were slowly making their way into the pool. With Ebony's persistence, Dre joined them.

As the crowd dwindled even more, Dre kicked it with his sister, her friend Mya and a few other people. Then he and Ebony fell into their own conversation, catching up on all the years they missed.

Their reminiscing was cut short when Dre saw her step through the door. Ebony followed his gaze, failing to understand what was occurring.

It was close to midnight. Hesitantly, Monica stood still, staring in his direction. Dre overheard the conversation she had with Eric.

"Dre is busy right now. Why don't you try to holla at him some other time?"

"He don't look too busy to me. Eric, please, I really need to talk to him. Please."

Eric hunched his shoulders, threw his hands up and looked over at Dre with Ebony.

"Seems as though I'm not the only one who has

some unfinished business with you, baby," Ebony whispered to him.

All the stress-filled, lonely days and nights never prepared him for the onslaught of emotions that accompanied the sight of Monica. She was still as beautiful as ever. His mind went back in time to when she meant the world to him, when he thought they would be together forever. His mind quickly fast-forwarded to her leaving him when he was locked down and couldn't give anymore.

Monica stood in front of them for what seemed like hours before speaking. Even then she failed to acknowledge Ebony.

"Hello, Dre," she said in her most seductive voice.

Silence.

"Dre?"

With eyes blazing, he spoke. "What's up, Mo? Surprised to see you here."

"I only stopped by to holla at you for a quick minute. I hope you don't mind."

In an attempt to control his rising anger, Dre exhaled slowly. "What you should be hoping is that my lady don't feel disrespected by your rudeness. You're interrupting our flow. Especially since you never acknowledged her."

His words put Ebony at ease as she accepted Monica's apology and greeting, somewhat understanding the situation.

Eric intervened. "Is everything OK over here?"

"Yeah, I got this, man."

"Aight, but I don't want no shit poppin' off," Eric said as he walked away.

"Me and her ain't got shit to talk about," Dre answered, a little harsher than intended.

"Dre, can I speak to you for a moment?"

"Listen, bit—um, Monica. I don't know what type of shit you on but you just need to back it up and leave 'cause I ain't tryin' to hear it," Dre said, raising his voice.

"Let me tell yo' ass one thing, Dre. Don't *ever* step to me like that again. I'm trying to respect you by wanting to talk to you in private, but shit, what I have to say can be said right here."

Ebony sensed the tension and excused herself to the bathroom.

"Nah you ain't gotta go nowhere. She ain't nobody," he said, pulling Ebony back over to him.

"It's OK. You need to handle this." She smiled, letting him know she was good.

Once Ebony was out of earshot, Dre unleashed all the pent up resentment for Monica that he'd held inside for so long.

"Bitch, you ain't got a muthafuckin' thing to say to me, you dig? For the last five years you ain't had shit to say, so let's keep it that way!"

"Dre, go ahead. Yell. Hell, curse me out if you want

to if that's gon' make you feel better. 'Cause when you get done ain't nothing gon' stop me from saying what the fuck I got to say," Monica retorted. Dre's temper had gotten the best of him and veins started popping out on his forehead, a sure sign he was over his limit. When he noticed his five-carat diamond cut chain and Cobra head medallion with sapphire eyes hanging from Monica's neck, he lost it. In one swift turn of his wrist, he grabbed the chain and twisted it around his hand, snatching her toward him.

"You think I'm something to play with? Give me my shit, bitch!"

Dee Dee and Eric had been watching the events unfold and both rushed to Monica's aid.

"DeAndre! DeAndre! Leave that girl alone!" his sister screamed as she ran toward them. She tried to break the hold that her brother had on Monica but she was much too weak.

"Leave that bullshit alone man! It's old, let it die," Eric yelled as he firmly grabbed Dre and pulled him away from her.

"I'm cool man! I'm cool," Dre responded as he stood back.

With tears streaming down her face, Monica stood before Dre. Disgusted at the sight of her in front of him, he stormed out of the yard and into the wooded area behind the house.

Acting upon instinct, Monica ran after him. Once

she caught up with him, she reached out and grabbed the bottom of his shirt. He turned around and saw her standing face to face with him. *This bitch is crazy*, he thought.

Before he was able to open his mouth and get a syllable out, she spoke. "Now that you've said what was on your mind, it's my turn!"

Feeling that his anger was about to get the best of him, he had to distance himself from her. Dre walked over to the hammock hanging between two oak trees and sat in it.

"What could you possibly have to say to me?" he yelled. "That you're sorry for deserting a nigga when he was on lock? Now you expect me to act like everything is cool? It ain't gonna happen. I fell for trying to make sure that both of us were straight, not just me. And what did you do? You gave me your ass to kiss. You might as well save that bullshit 'cause I ain't tryin' to hear it!"

She looked hard into his eyes as she sat beside him. "Yes, I do want to say that I'm sorry for not being there for you. I was young and afraid of being alone. I thought of all the lonely nights I spent waiting on you to come home and all the different women I used to see with you." She wiped the tears from her eyes. "But when I realized that nothing or nobody could replace you, it was too late and I didn't know how to come back, Dre."

At that very moment, he felt her heartache but his

pride wouldn't let him compromise with the promise that he had made to himself up in those walls.

"Where's all my shit at, Mo?"

She lifted the chain from around her neck and handed him the pouch that was clutched in her hand. "Here, these are yours. Everything is where and how you left it," she answered. "I wanted to give you this but I also wanted to ask for your forgiveness." She squatted down in front of him, resting her arms in his lap. "Please forgive me, Dre."

Not liking the feelings he felt, he stood up and moved her away. "OK Mo," he said as he let out a deep breath. "Thanks, but it's time I got back to my company."

"Is that your girl, DeAndre?"

"That's none of your business."

"Well, when you get the chance, will you at least come see me?"

They stood and looked into each other's eyes, saying nothing. Finally, Monica turned to leave, deciding not to address the question because they both knew the answer. Instead, she kissed him on the cheek and left.

Dre's mind was in a whirlwind as he made it back to the party. Everyone was gone. Eric and Trina were naked in the pool while Ebony sat on the side with her feet dangling in the water. She was lost in her own thoughts, paying them no mind. She smiled as she saw Dre appear. He sat next to her while she made no com-

ment about the episode with Monica.

"Are you all right, baby?" she asked as she slowly rubbed his back.

"I am now," he replied with a genuine smile on his face. Ebony's acceptance of things for what they were was what he admired most about her.

They talked a while longer. She made sure he knew everyone made mistakes, at one point or another, in life. After watching Trina and Eric in the pool, Ebony beamed a seductive smile.

"You wanna join them?"

"After you." He followed her into the water.

With all the lights off except those in the pool, they enjoyed each other, eventually shedding their clothes as well. Once in, he grabbed her from the back and pulled her against his body. He wrapped his arms around her, caressing her breasts and sliding his hands between her legs. Trina wasn't bashful about walking around naked. She was a dime and she knew it. She was in and out of the pool, making sure their drinks were full. Ebony watched Trina move about as Dre was feeling her up. She couldn't believe they were together again. She turned to face Dre and they stared into each other's eyes then kissed passionately. Dre never imagined coming home to such sweetness so soon. Before the night was over, Ebony lost her shyness as well.

TWO

Dee Dee stood in the bathroom of Rich's North Side condo with an ice pack held to her eye. He appeared in the doorway.

"I'm gon' ask you one more muthafuckin' time. Where the fuck you been, Dee Dee?"

"How many times do I have to tell you? Unlike you, I don't sleep around, Rich! I wasn't with no damn man! I was at my brother's party. But regardless of where I was, it don't give you no reason to put your hands on me!"

He closed the distance between them quickly, grabbing her around the neck. "Let me tell you one thing, bitch!" He brought her ear close to his mouth. "As long as you spending my damn money, I want to know *where*

the fuck you at, *what* the fuck you doin' and *who* the fuck you with! Do you understand me?" he hissed, pushing her away from him.

Dee Dee stormed into the bedroom. Determined that this was the last time he would put his hands on her, she began packing her bags.

"Don't try to flip this shit around! That's the one thing I can't stand about yo' lying, cheating, no good ass. You can do all the dirt in the world but can't stand to think of the same thing happening to you! Well let me tell you something, muthafucka! You don't own me and those couple of dollars you got in yo' pockets don't give you the right to put yo' hands on me!"

Rich stood at the bar with a double shot of Rémy to his lips. His bloodshot eyes watched her as she stormed around the room. He downed the drink in one swallow before speaking. "Bitch, while you running your goddamn mouth, you better respect who the fuck you talking to and recognize the hand that feeds your ass!"

"You think 'cause you got some money you rule the world. Money don't make you no man, nigga! It only makes a bigger trick," she spat as she picked up her bags, heading toward the door.

As she reached for the doorknob, Rich threw his shot glass. It barely missed Dee Dee's head. "Dick sucking bitch!"

"Yeah, but I'm a good one, trick!" she screamed as she walked out of the door, slamming it behind her.

Dee Dee had driven all over the South Side of Chicago, trying to clear her head, before finally deciding to stop in Hyde Park. She found a nice, quiet spot looking out over Lake Michigan and parked. As she sat there listening to the slow, soothing sounds of WGCI, she flipped the sun visor down and looked at her eye. She knew she would not to be able to hide the black and blue bruise from Dre.

"Bitch-ass nigga!" she screamed to herself as she slammed her fists against the dashboard.

She reclined in her seat, wishing she had taken her friend up on his invitation to spend the night together after Dre's welcome home party.

It was 3:30 in the morning when the police car came to a halt behind her brand new Acura. She was sound asleep. After he ran the tag, he approached the car with caution, not knowing whether the occupant was armed, injured or dead. With the butt of his gun, he tapped the window.

Dee Dee jumped awake instantly, reaching for the .380 pistol she carried in the driver's door side pocket. After she saw that it was a police officer, she relaxed, slowly releasing her grip on her strap.

Her unexpected movement caused the officer to raise his pistol. He instructed her to put her hands in the air. It wasn't until he evaluated the situation that he eased his gun back into its holster. "Young lady, are you

aware that this area is off limits to patrons after 1 o'clock? It's also extremely dangerous for anyone, let alone a woman, to be asleep in a car this time of morning."

"I apologize, sir. I must have dozed off. Maybe I should be on my way," she said, looking at the officer for the first time.

He cringed at the sight of her face. "It seems as though you have enough problems already without having to worry about me writing you a loitering ticket, Mrs. Smith," he said, shaking his head. "I presume that is your name, right?"

She nodded in response to his question.

"Would you like to go to the hospital or file a complaint?" The officer spoke with his voice full of concern and compassion.

"Look, Officer umm…"

"Daniels." He finished for her.

"Officer Daniels, I had a minor accident. It's nothing," she tried to reassure him. "I just came here to clear my head and I dozed off. OK? I'm all right and I really need to be going."

"Mrs. Smith—"

"It's Miss. I'm not married. My name is Deidre."

"Well, Deidre, is it worth it?"

"Is what worth it?" She knew what he was hinting around at, but her defensiveness got in the way of being fully aware of the situation at hand.

"Oh! I get it now. You love him so much that you're willing to protect him. He blacked your eye, so what's next, huh? Next time he'll break your arm or blow your brains out. I guess that's cool too, right?"

The tone of his voice and the curl of his lips into a smirk told her that he had dealt with situations like these before. She decided to come clean. "No, Officer Daniels, that's not cool, but I'm not trying to get the police all up in my business. I can take care of this myself," she answered, returning his same smirk.

He found her reasoning, strength and beauty alluring but wanted to make sure she understood the results of domestic violence above anything else. "You deserve better, Miss Smith. There are plenty of men who would respect and cherish a woman as beautiful as you are." He leaned farther into her car.

Dee Dee couldn't help but smile at his weak-ass line. "And you just so happen to be one of the many, right? Is that through trial and error or what?"

"You can say that. I was raised in an abusive household, so I got to give Ma Dukes some credit for rising above," he said as he smiled, showing a mouth full of beautiful white teeth. "Not to contradict my reason for stopping, but perhaps you'll give me the chance to show you how a woman should be treated."

"I can't believe this. I look like shit, my eye's all messed up, and here you are flirting with me, knowing I got a man. Wouldn't that be considered…cheat-

ing…from a man's perspective?" Her smile revealed that she wasn't offended.

He burst out laughing, knowing that what she said was true.

"Does that make me a corrupt cop?" he asked.

"That's for you to answer, Mister…"

"Anthony. Tony for short."

"OK, Tony, but you need to stick to the script here, and your own kind, someone more your speed like a lawyer or something," Deidre said, smiling.

"Hold up shorty, don't let the uniform fool you. I grew up in the ghetto. Cabrini-Green to be exact. So don't judge a book by its cover."

She could never imagine going out with a police officer, but here she was, entertaining the thought. She turned to face him, their lips only inches apart.

"So, what's it gonna be?" He handed her his card.

"Look, Tony, I can't make any promises, but I'll think about it. OK? I need to get myself together, so I'll have to get back with you."

Tony rose up off the car, accepting her answer. "That's cool." He turned to walk away then stopped as though pondering something. "Oh, yeah, one more thing before you go."

"Yeah, what's that?"

"I need to see your driver's license."

The look she gave him made him double over laughing.

"I'm just fuckin' with you. But I am dead serious about seeing you again."

"No. You're not fuckin' with me. You are conversing with me. There's a difference," she said as she started her car.

"You got me. On the real though, holla at yo' boy."

"We'll see, Tony," she said then pulled off.

"You do have a license, don't you?" he hollered as she drove past him. She waved, never answering his question.

Dre and Ebony rose with the sun, making love. She was due to leave later that day. The rekindled passion between them was so strong. They made sure the other was completely satisfied before joining Eric and Trina for breakfast.

The two couples sat around the table talking while eating hash browns, eggs and turkey bacon. Once the girls started to clean up, Dre and E went into the den to smoke a blunt.

"E-Mo, I had a blast last night, homie," Dre said as he put his arm around his partna.

"That ain't nothing, homeboy. I told you before I left that we was gon' be all right. As long as we keep our shit in order and don't make any crazy moves, we gon' be all right."

"Fo' sho'!"

"And you definitely can't be trippin' like you were

last night! What's really happening with you, playa? That broad said she had something to give you." Eric laughed at Dre. "Matter of fact, I got something to give you, too, but don't try that shit with me, nigga. I bar none," E said jokingly as he left the room.

Dre sat there thinking about the night before, listening to Ebony and Trina in the other room, wondering what else E had in store for him.

Eric returned, carrying a large Gucci bag. He tossed the bag at Dre who caught it. "What is this, man?"

"Something to get you on your feet, playboy."

Bewildered, he opened the bag. Inside was a stack of bills totaling fifty thousand dollars and a set of car keys. Dre looked at his partna, aghast. "Nigga, I got mad love for you!" He held the keys in the air. "What's up with these?"

"Come on and find out," E said, walking toward the garage.

Once at the garage, E opened the first of three doors, walked over to the car and snatched the cover off. Dre was speechless when he saw the Dodge Viper in his favorite color. The natural light coming into the garage glimmered as it hit the candy-coated sapphire blue paint job. Dre opened the door to sink into the piped out cream and blue bucket seat that easily adjusted to his contour. The grip of the cherry wood grain steering wheel assured him that it was time to reclaim his glory and take his rightful place on the streets of the Chi.

"It's time to retire the Mustang." E appeared in the doorway, enjoying his partna's surprise. "You good to go with the temporary tag for a minute. It's in my dealer's name." Eric crossed his arms with confidence, knowing Dre would put it down properly.

Ebony's flight was due out of O'Hare at 4:30 p.m., so around noon, they said their goodbyes to Eric and Trina. They decided it would be good to use the two-hour drive to the airport to get reacquainted. However, their ride was solemn, affected strongly by the sadness of Ebony's imminent departure. They spoke very few words.

With the top down and the wind blowing through her hair, Ebony's eyes hid behind the tint of her Gucci shades. She sat motionless, and he could sense her anguish.

"Ebony, you all right?"

"Yeah, I'm cool." Her smile belied her mood. "I only wish that things were different with us. That so much time wouldn't have to pass between us seeing each other again. Last time was so frustrating for me. I know your plate is full, and I don't want to pressure you. Just don't ever forget that if you need me, I'm here, just a telephone call away."

"It ain't a question in my mind about that, baby. I just need a little time and things gon' get better for us."

"I'm holding you to that," she said, placing her

hand on his thigh.

"That's my word."

Inside the airport, they sat in the lounge area, listening to music as they waited on Ebony's assignment. Even in her uniform she was sexy. Dre kept his hands attached to her as if she would disappear if he let her go. When their time was up, they embraced, not wanting to break the bond. With tears falling from Ebony's hazel eyes, Dre kissed them away and promised that they would be together again, soon. Walking away, the grasp of their hands could no longer keep them connected. Ebony stepped away. She couldn't turn around to look at Dre, one last time, before she boarded her flight.

On the drive back into the city, Dre's mind started playing tricks on him. He thought every car was the police. He really tripped out after he remembered the temporary tag and the money in the trunk. "Fuck it," he said and fired up a blunt to relax.

He exhaled a sigh of relief when he pulled into his sister's driveway. Glancing at Dee Dee's car as he entered through the garage, he wondered about the guy she left the party with last night and if that was Rich he saw her talking to.

"Dee Dee, you home?" he called from the kitchen.

There was no answer.

He climbed the stairs and called her name again.

Once he got to her bedroom door, he put his ear up to it to see if she had company. He heard nothing but silence. He jarred the door and peeked in. A smile crept across his face as he saw her in bed, sound asleep. He closed the door and headed for the shower.

That was close, Deidre thought to herself.

Dre emerged from the steamy bathroom with a towel wrapped around his waist and water droplets shimmering across his back. He went back to his room totally exhausted from the last twenty-four hours but also relaxed from the shower. He had almost dozed off when he remembered the pouch Monica had given him. He opened it.

After counting the seventy-five hundred dollars, he found a note that read:

Dre,

I don't know what the future holds for us, but I do know that my love for you has never wavered, even when my trust did. Even when we weren't together physically, we were together spiritually. I never loved another as I do you. I hope that you can find it in your heart to forgive me.

Monica

He read the note again and lay back on the bed. Staring at the ceiling, he had thoughts of their past. Ebony's face appeared and brought him back to reality. He cursed himself, wishing he didn't think of Monica so much.

Getting up to retrieve some lotion from the bath-

room, he noticed the door was locked. He didn't see Dee Dee as she crept past while he was engaged in a mental tug-of-war. Dee Dee was startled when she opened the door to find Dre.

"Hey, what's up, sis?"

She turned her head quickly.

"What the fuck?" He grabbed her face and turned it toward him. Getting an up close and personal view of the black and blue bruise on the side of her face, he barked, "What the fuck is wrong with your eye, girl! I know muthafuckin' well you ain't let some nigga punch you. Who the fuck did that? Rich?"

"It was an accident," Dee Dee whispered, almost as if apologizing for him. But her eyes told the truth.

He felt disrespected like he was the one wearing the bruise. It wasn't the mere fact that it was his sister but the condition she was in. He took a closer look at her face. "Was it the guy at the party last night?"

"No. Dre, don't get involved in my business. I can handle my own."

Dre exploded. "You obviously can't! Look at your face!" he said, forcing her to look in the mirror. As tears fell from her eyes, his tone softened. "You are my business." Holding her close to his chest, he continued, "And you can tell that bitch-ass nigga who did that, I'm going to see him." After his promise was made, loud and clear, Dre walked away to make a phone call.

"I'm not seeing him anymore," she said to herself

since he was long gone.

Dre was on the phone talking to E, explaining the incident. Eric gave him the run down on dude, suggesting that Dre should not make a big deal out of it. Rich was known to go all out and E didn't feel this situation warranted such drastic measures, especially when they had bigger and better issues to worry about than a nigga checking his broad.

"Man, this ain't no damn hoe check, this my sister! You haven't seen her muthafuckin' eye. Yeah, I know shit gon' happen, but you don't punch no broad in the eye like she a nigga!"

"Dre, you of all people should understand, especially the way you were caught up in your emotions last night. So I guess Monica's people should be beefing with you, feel me?" E knew that Dre was stubborn. He just wanted him to think more rationally.

"Man, I ain't trying to hear that bullshit! I ain't do half the shit I wanted to do. I know I got off my square a lil' bit, but I didn't hit that bitch with no right hook either. If I let a nigga disrespect mines like that, I might as well put a skirt on too, and you *know* that ain't happening!"

"Check this out, I know you want to straighten this shit out but at the same time, respect it. You know I'm down with you, right or wrong, but think about what you got to lose."

Dre thought about the implications of beefin' with

someone so soon after his release and understood where Eric was coming from. He had a lot to take care of in terms of getting back on his feet, but he wasn't about to compromise his integrity at his sister's expense. He didn't know Rich or what he was about, but he had to handle the Negro to let him know that his sister was not a punching bag.

THREE

Over the next few weeks, Eric took Dre under his wing and schooled him on how the game was different since the last time he was on the streets. Things had changed over the last five years and he wanted his boy to be on top of his shit, especially on the repercussions of unplanned moves. Once he was confident, he gave Dre a kilo of heroin to flip. He told him to put a six on the dope. Dre followed Eric's instructions and the one kilo turned into six while the money was crazy. In a matter of weeks, Dre had over two hundred thousand dollars.

Dre wasn't trying to see Monica but he made a special trip to visit Ebony. Although the visit was more for pleasure, he installed a safe at her place. His feelings for

her had grown, and he believed he could trust her.

Dee Dee's eye finally went down, allowing her to venture out in search of space for a hair salon. Dre promised that she would have no more worries. He also told her to not see Rich ever again, under any circumstances. She knew that would be hard and decided not to mention his daily calls, trying to convince her to meet with him so they could talk. She found it difficult rejecting him, after all the years of following his orders, but she sensed the propensity for violence between the two. She knew that continuing to see him would provoke a deadly altercation between Dre and Rich.

Having witnessed the influence Dre possessed over his crew as well as the way that he could hold a grudge against someone, she wanted them to avoid bumping heads. But she knew that was next to impossible. She knew it was just a matter of time before they crossed paths. Then there were the plans she made to spend time with Tony over the holiday. That made her nervous, too.

♦ ♦ ♦

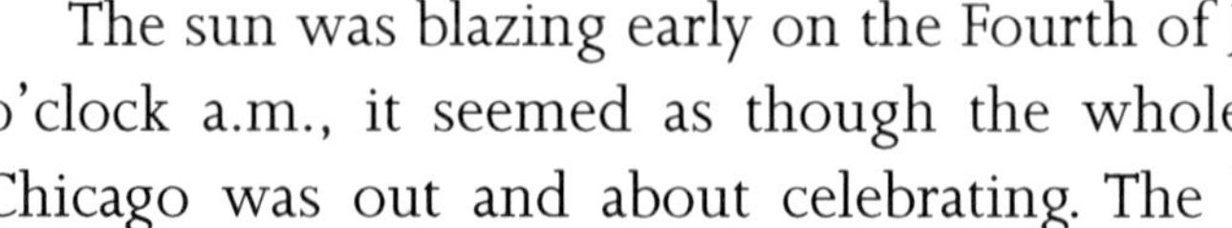

The sun was blazing early on the Fourth of July. At 9 o'clock a.m., it seemed as though the whole city of Chicago was out and about celebrating. The beaches, parks and basketball courts along Lake Shore Drive were packed like a suitcase full of money. As Dre sat behind the tint of the Viper, enjoying the euphoria of the blunt held in his mouth, he nodded his head to the sounds of Biggie's "*Fuck You Tonight*" as it blasted out of the Bose system. He approached the 31st Street exit but came to a stop because traffic was backed up. He was about to call to check on his crew when a G500, filled with women, pulled up next to him. The women were admiring his ride and the driver motioned for him to let the window down.

After cracking the glass, letting the smoke escape into the summer's breeze, he spoke. "What's up, ma?"

"That's what we tryna find out, Mr. DeAndre," the driver quickly responded.

Damn, how the fuck she know my name? he thought to himself. Suddenly, a familiar face appeared from the passenger's side. It was Trina. A slight chuckle escaped his lips as he smiled. "What's happening, Trina?"

"The picnic, Dre. I hope you're headed that way." She seductively licked her lips.

"I hope so, too," one of the girls in the back seat commented. "Because that weed smells good as a muthafucka!"

Dre smiled. "Don't trip, I got plenty where this came from and yeah, we going to the same spot," he responded as he puffed on the Optimo some more.

"Good," the driver said as traffic begin to move. "I'm looking forward to getting to know you better."

Dre never acknowledged her comment; instead, catching a break in the traffic, he floored the Viper, disappearing down the exit.

Once he arrived, he found a good parking space.

Seemed like everyone was already there. The G500 pulled in next to him while Trina jumped out and slid in his car. As she sat down, her mini dress rode up around her waist. She turned to face him, giving him an unobstructed view of her pussy. "Let me hit that," she said, taking the blunt out of his mouth. With a long drag, she continued. "Look Dre, I'm gonna get straight to the point because I know you ain't crazy. When are you going to give me some of that dick that I been trying to get since you came home?" She spread her legs even wider. Her pubic hairs were neatly trimmed and her pussy lips were meaty.

Dre sat back, staring at her, disbelieving her boldness. He decided to give it to her straight up with no cut. "Check this out, Trina. You and me go way back, for real. You my girl and all but you also my man's woman and I don't get down like that." Her eyes rolled to the back of her head as if she couldn't believe she was being turned down. Dre continued, "I'm saying, it ain't no question that you fine as a muthafucka, but at the same time, you know that won't bring nothing but problems." His eyes were fixated on the mound that rested in between her legs. The sight of her pussy and the mere thought of running up in her caused his dick to rise. She noticed the erection.

"Looks like somebody else seems to think otherwise," she said as she ran her hand across his dick.

He never flinched. "Ain't no shame in my game. I'm

a man before anything else, but I ain't trying to go there with you, Trina." He cut off the car, opened his door and walked toward the barbeque. Trina shook her head and adjusted her clothes as she watched him walk away.

The smell of ribs, chicken and steaks on the grill wafted through the air as Dre made his way to the pavilion that they had reserved. E's customized Ford Lightning sat in plain view as his system had everyone nodding to 2Pac's "*How Do You Want It*."

E, Mookie and Lil Greg, Dre's childhood friends, sat around playing dominoes and talking shit to each other. Most of the women were cooking. Others were dancing, laughing and doing their own thing.

Toi, the driver of the G500, had her eyes on Dre since the traffic jam. She was secretly excited that they were going to the same place. She spotted him and was ready to make a move. Swaying to the beat of the music, she approached Dre with two Coronas in her hands. She moved provocatively as she gave Dre a beer. Seductively, she eased between his legs and proceeded to entertain him with a slow and erotic lap dance. Dre had already made up his mind that he was fuckin' her that night. Biggie had said it best.

It was like déjà vu when he looked up and saw Monica approaching from the parking lot. He let out a sigh, hypnotized by her beauty. Her bronze skin radiated in the summer's heat while a halter top, skin-tight

denim Bermuda shorts and Prada heels complemented her physique very well. With that visual in sight Dre had no choice but to push Toi out the way.

Monica's approach was interrupted as she stopped to allow a canary yellow 500SL to pass. Rich, with his partna, Nine, came to a halt beside her and extended an invitation to join them. Dre didn't know that the driver of the car was Rich. Even so, he was still relieved to see her brush them off and continue walking toward the pavilion. As they cruised by, they nodded in his direction.

"Cuz riding real decent," Dre commented to no one in particular.

"That's that nigga Rich, the one your sister fucks with," Mookie said nonchalantly, not knowing the effect his words would have upon Dre.

"Is that so?" Dre was even more interested now. His eyes followed the car and watched the crowd gather around it as Rich parked. His first instinct was to go straighten the nigga out about his sister, but the thought quickly vanished as Monica's voice reached him.

"Hello, DeAndre. What's up, fellas?"

Dre looked into her eyes for a moment before he responded. "What's up, Mo?"

Monica cut her eyes at Toi who was still standing close to Dre. "Not as good as you are I see, but I'm cool." Looking between the two of them, she continued, "Looks like you aren't wasting any time getting back into the groove of things, huh?"

"What it looks like is that you're worried about the wrong thing." His eyes bored into hers.

"Well, first of all, I'm not worried. Secondly, if you have a problem with me being here, perhaps I should leave."

Dre watched as she turned to walk away. She took a few steps before he spoke again. "You know it ain't even like that."

E nudged Mookie and the rest of the crew, motioning for them to give Dre and Monica some room to iron out their differences.

Monica stopped and turned back to face him. "What is it like then, Dre?"

"Come over here and let me tell you about it." When she stood in front of him he continued. "Mo, you know something, as much as I hate to admit it, you've been on my mind a lot lately. I'm glad to see you. It's just been hectic trying to get things back in order, you know."

She stood staring at him with a smirk on her face. "I understand that Dre, but you need to be trying to take care of your business right here. I've made it perfectly clear that I regret the things I did and want to spend some time with you. We all make mistakes."

He found his anger toward her easing. He reached for her hand and pulled her closer to him. Her body did not resist and she stood in between his legs where Toi

had just been. He ran his hands down her back then rested them on her ass. As his hands made their way up the leg of her shorts, caressing her behind, she leaned into him. The intimacy brought back a thousand memories.

"Hey, Dre," Mookie called out.

As Dre and Monica turned in his direction, a series of about four or five photos were taken with them wrapped in each other's arms.

"That ought to be one for the archives," Mookie said, laughing.

Monica was smiling from ear to ear. Dre just shook his head.

"Ya'll trying to hit the jet skis with the rest of us or are there more…uh…pressing matters at hand?" E asked, winking his eye.

Dre looked at Mo. "What's up? You feel like taking a ride with me?"

"You know I do." She moved closer to him, instinctively grinding her pulsating pussy against his dick. "Although I don't think we are talking about the same kind of riding, I guess this will do for right now."

Monica looked in Dre's eyes and brushed her lips across his, barely touching them. Feeling his erection at its fullest peak, she caressed it with her hand. "I need to be sliding over something else besides water before the night is over. It's been a minute."

"How long has it been?" He regretted the words

before they escaped his mouth. "Never mind, don't answer that." He pushed her away.

"C'mon Dre, don't start. We're having a good time. Let's leave the past exactly where it's at—in the past."

His mood had changed almost instantly. "Yeah, you're absolutely right. Come on, let's go."

Mookie pulled up in his Harley Davidson truck with the skis and they hopped in the bed of the pickup. Monica was under Dre as if she was his woman again, thinking he would eventually come around and back to her. She touched and caressed him, hoping he would overlook her abandonment.

A couple of hours passed and everyone enjoyed themselves, acting like big kids at the park. The tension between Dre and Monica had worn off and they called it a truce for the moment.

He rode behind her, taking advantage of the easy access to her body. At one point, away from everyone else, he lifted her top to expose her breasts. She became so caught up and aroused with him playing with her nipples that she lost control and they fell into the water. They laughed and held on to each other. Monica was happy because it was like old times.

Dee Dee made it to the picnic a little past noon. She saw the cars but had yet to spot anybody she knew. Had she seen Rich staring at her in the distance, she would've left. Although Tony's persistence won her over,

she wasn't prepared for her brother's reaction to seeing her with another man, any man. Even she had trouble getting over what happened to her at the hands of Rich, and wasn't ready to venture back to the unknown—even if it was just a friendship. Yet, Tony was attractive, and she enjoyed his conversation. Most of all, she didn't believe he had any ulterior motives, so she agreed to allow him to meet her at the picnic.

Once Rich spotted Dee Dee, he dropped everything he was doing and headed in her direction. At the same time, Tony parked a couple of spaces down from her, and arrived at her car just ahead of Rich. She was surprised when she opened her door and saw him standing there.

Tony looked good wearing Maurice Malone jean shorts, leather sandals and a T-shirt. She looked at him from head to toe and a chill ran down her spine from the thought of him butt-ass naked.

"Hi, Tony," she said with a smile on her face that revealed her thoughts.

"What's up, Deidre," he responded. "I was hoping you would be a little more excited to see me."

"Why you say that?"

"'Cause you ain't gave a nigga a hug or nothing."

"You know I don't have a problem giving you a hug as good as you look!" She stepped out of the car, smoothed her sundress down in the back and leaped into his arms without hesitation.

As he embraced her, he savored the smell of her hair and perfume. "Damn, this feels good," he whispered in her ear.

"I was about to say the same thing," she said as she closed her eyes, enjoying the feel of his body.

As she opened her eyes to look up at Tony, her body froze. She saw Rich standing in front of her. His eyes were blazing.

Tony felt her body tense and turned around to see what had her vexed. Not knowing what was going on, he asked, "What's good? You got a problem or something?"

"Yeah, but it ain't nothing like it's gon' be if you don't mind your muthafuckin' business!" Rich spoke menacingly and Tony felt challenged. "I'm tryna holla at my woman if that's all right with you."

Dee Dee rolled her eyes. She couldn't have asked to be more embarrassed. "Rich, I ain't your woman and we ain't got shit to talk about. I'm busy." Her voice held more passion than aggression.

Her comment knocked Rich clear off his square. He could never get used to being denied by her or accept the fact that she wasn't his woman. After raising her for so many years, he felt like he owned her. He stepped close to her and she could smell the alcohol on his breath.

"Didn't I say I'm tryna holla at you?"

She placed her hands on his chest and gently pushed

him out of her face. "Yeah, and I said we don't have shit to talk about, so gon' head with the bullshit, Rich!"

Tony stepped in at that moment. "Ay, didn't she say that she didn't want to be bothered? Take yo' ass on and go sweat one of these other broads."

Rich never acknowledged Tony. Instead, he continued to focus on Dee Dee. "Bitch, don't grandstand in front of this nigga! Everything you own I bought. You think it's a game?"

Dee Dee grabbed Tony's hand, trying to walk away from the situation.

"Bitch, I bought you. I own you, you money hungry trick. And for you, ebony man," he snarled, looking at Tony from head to toe. "Have fun with her, but just know, I'm loaning the bitch out to you. Maybe we can make some payment arrangements. She'll do anything for the that almighty dollar." This time, Rich laughed heartily.

"Nigga, have you—"

"Stop! It ain't worth it!" she yelled at Tony, grabbing his arm as he fought to get at Rich.

"Yeah nigga, listen to that bitch 'fore you fuck around and get yo' ass beat!"

Tony's anger was about to take over, but there was something in the way that stopped him from hitting Rich.

The words, *it ain't worth it*, continued to echo in his head. He looked down and saw Dee Dee speaking the

words. She continued to plead with him, trying to convince him that an altercation wasn't worth the trouble. She also knew that although Tony was a cop, he was in over his head fuckin' with a lunatic like Rich. "Tony, it's cool. Don't pay him no mind. It's funny he keep bringing his no good ass around. Let's just go enjoy ourselves."

On the way back to the picnic area, everyone was oblivious to what was going down. It was a stroke of luck that Monica glanced ahead and noticed a small crowd gathered in the parking lot. After a closer look, she spotted Dee Dee. "Dre, ain't that your sister?" she asked.

"Where at?" He followed her gaze and saw Rich's hand in his sister's face. He jumped out of the truck running before his feet could hit the ground. Dodging cars, he snatched the Desert Eagle out of his waist.

"Nigga, this ain't for you! It's personal and you ought to be glad, but next time you get in my business, I'm gonna blow your brains out," Rich told Tony as he pulled the .380 Beretta out of the small of his back.

The situation had indeed turned ugly. Dee Dee knew Rich meant each and every word. This time when he approached her, she kept quiet. "You think it's as simple as that, Dee Dee? Well, it ain't like that, bitch," he said, poking her in the face with the pistol.

Dre crept like a panther through the parked cars. Nobody saw him. It was pure instinct and reflexes that

caused Rich to flinch and avoid the full impact of Dre's swing. Although he missed the blunt of the blow, it was still enough to throw him off balance. Dre, like a man possessed, pistol-whipped Rich. In his drunken state, he was no match for Dre. At the same time, he wasn't going down without a fight. He lunged at Dre, trying to catch him off-guard but Dre was in rare form. His adrenaline was high and he was filled with rage. He caught Rich flush in the mouth with his knee, knocking out his front teeth.

The screams and pleas from the gathering crowd went unheard as Dre closed in for the kill. It was then that Rich's partna, Nine, appeared holding two chrome-plated, rubber-gripped nine millimeter pistols, aimed at Dre's head.

Believe that Nine didn't get his name from faking. He was always strapped, and it was no secret that he would empty his clips at the drop of a dime.

"Yo Dre! Behind you!" Someone hollered a warning that caused him to look Nine's way.

"Pop this fool, cuz," Rich sputtered as he wiped blood from his mouth.

Under any other circumstances, Dre would have been dead in a matter of moments, but the crowd caused Nine to hesitate. That split second was enough time for E, Mookie and the rest of the crew to reach Dre. Mookie jumped the curb and came to a screeching halt like the Dukes of Hazzard. He leaned out of the driver's side door of the truck with an AR-15 aimed at Nine's head. "One more step and you late," Mookie said. The potential for an assault rifle battle caused most of the onlookers to scatter, not wanting to catch a stray bullet.

Nine froze. His eyes roamed over the many guns aimed at him and Rich. A wicked and vicious grin spread across his face as he realized, at that moment, that the odds were stacked against him. He decided to live and fight another day.

Rich stood beside Nine, his eyes staring intently at Dee Dee as he passed her. "You mark-ass niggas willing to put your life on the line for this backstabbing bitch? The graveyard is full of stupid muthafuckas just like ya'll!"

"Fuck you, Rich!" Dee Dee screamed.

"Consider yourself fucked!" Rich shot back.

"Dee, go get in the car!" Dre yelled.

"I'm not leaving you here, Dre!"

Dre looked at Tony and they exchanged mental messages.

"He's right, Dee. Let's go." Tony took her by the hand and led her away from the scene.

"Nigga, if you got a problem with what I did, deal with it because next time you put your hands on my sister, one of us gon' die!"

Recognition set in on Rich's face. He realized that nigga trying to punk him was Dee Dee's brother.

"Oh shit! It's good ole Dre…back home from the

joint," Rich joked.

"Yeah I'm back. You touch my sister again—"

"You what nigga? You didn't seem to have a problem while I took care of her for the six years you were gone."

To send a message that he was the wrong nigga to fuck with, Dre contemplated poppin' him right in front of everyone then he remembered when Eric said, "*Think about what you got to lose.*"

The police sirens were distant, but enough warning for the crowd to disperse. Rich and Nine quickly disappeared into the crowd, knowing that things were far from over.

Dee Dee left her car with Dre and rode with Tony. Monica and Dre stood off to the side.

"You alright?" she asked.

"Yeah I'm cool."

"So what's up? You gon' stop by later?"

He looked at her perplexed. "Was you not just standing here? Can't you see I got a lot on my mind right now?"

"I got a lot on my mind, too," she said as she nibbled on his bottom lip and pulled him into her body.

"Mo, please, not right now. I'll see what I can do but I ain't makin' no promises," Dre said as he walked away, rubbing his hands across his face. He tried to wash away the event that had just unfolded.

Accepting defeat, she reflected on how she treated

him when he was locked up. "If you need me, I'm here," she assured. She finally left, uncertain of when she would see him again.

The fellas sat around, trying to figure out their next move. E broke the silence. "Man, this fucked up. If they think it's over, just like that, I got somethin' else for they ass!"

"Homie, I took what you said to heart about beefin' with that nigga. But if it takes me dying for my blood, then that's what time it is. However, I ain't tryna pull nobody else into my beef," Dre said.

Mookie was quiet the entire time. Even though he knew what type of shit Rich and Nine were on, he wasn't too eager to make peace. They bled the same as he did. Finally, he could hold his thoughts no longer. "Dre, your beef is our beef! We ain't ducking no rec with them bitch-ass niggas," he said with venom in his voice.

"Homeboy, we ain't never gonna let niggas disrespect us. All I'm saying is watch your back and don't get caught slippin'," E stated.

"Never that, homie! Never that!" Dre said, looking out over Lake Michigan.

It was well into the evening when they left the lakefront and plans were made to meet at E's crib the next morning.

FOUR

After taking a soothing hot shower, Dre stretched across Monica's bed, his brow furrowed as he relived the day's events. Monica studied him as she entered the room. She knew he had a lot on his mind but so did she—like how she planned to regain his trust, love and affection. Setting the baby oil and towel on the nightstand, she let her robe fall to the floor. The sight of her beautiful body always turned him on and that moment was no exception.

He closed his eyes as she poured the warm oil onto his chest. His problems seemed to fade away with each stroke. As she worked her way lower, his body responded with excitement and anxious anticipation. With each caress, she planted a kiss while exploring the length of

his body. She moaned as she put his dick into her mouth.

Dre positioned Monica so he could put his hands between her legs. She was already soaking wet, obviously excited as she grinded on his fingers. She poured all her excitement into pleasing him. As she climbed on top of him, her soft breasts bounced as he held her waist. He guided her onto his penis. Her back stiffened and a soft moan escaped her lips as she slid down the shaft of his dick.

"Oh, Dre! Dre! Dre!" Monica screamed. Their rhythm, slow at first, quickly increased as he bounced her up and down without reserve. Sweat ran between the cleavage of her titties, dripping on his chest as he enjoyed the pain he was inflicting upon her.

Dre didn't hesitate positioning her at the edge of the bed. He stood on the floor and entered her from behind. He poured all of the emotions he suffered over the years into each stroke. Although his stride was steady, she was enjoying it and making sounds that he had waited so long to hear. On the verge of cumming, he continued to pound into her with an almost violent abandonment. He pulled her back to meet his thrusts as he released himself inside of her vagina.

After they caught their breath, they fell on the bed and Dre reached over to pull her closer to him. She moved away from him.

"Stop! Don't touch me! You're a mad man," she said,

smiling, before sliding into his arms. She reached up and started kissing him on the neck. "Are you ready to come home, DeAndre?"

"Mo, I'm not trying to hear that right now, OK?"

She began nibbling on the left side of his neck and outlining his nipples with her fingers. "I'm serious, Dre," she said, ignoring his statement.

He reached for the blunt in the ashtray on the nightstand. He was an emotional wreck, not really understanding his feelings. All he knew was that he was being pulled in two different directions and had no idea which way to go.

Monica was persistent and wanted an answer from him. She turned his face toward her. "Did you hear me, Dre?"

"Didn't I tell you I'm not trying to hear that right now? I guess because we fucked everything is supposed to be all right and I'm expected to forget what happened between us."

"No! I know that you couldn't possibly forget or forgive me for doing the same thing you did while we were together! No, that's too much like right, ain't it?"

Dre stared at her. *Damn, she sure know how to fuck up a good nut*, he said to himself.

"Tell me something, DeAndre, how long are you gonna keep throwing this in my face before you just put this behind us?"

"Behind us my ass, Monica! Really! I shouldn't have

ever come here, but that's neither here nor there. We fucked! Big deal! It is what it is. Still, I ain't getting ready to invest my time and energy in a 'here one minute, gone the next minute' type of broad!"

"You really wanna go there, Dre? Do we need to talk about all the shit you used to do? What about all the different bitches? How about the nights you never came home? Do you remember that? Hell no! Of course you don't! Why? Because you too caught up in what I didn't do once you left. You didn't have to hustle then or now. You did it because you like easy money, and I don't knock you for that. In fact, I love you for it, but don't nothing last forever, Dre! What's after the hustle?"

Hearing her speak her mind caused him to pause and sit up in the bed. He gathered his thoughts before speaking. "I guess I shouldn't have no beef with you then, huh? You never really wanted to spend the grands you did on any and everything you wanted. You wanna complain now? It's funny because your ass never complained then. If I did fuck some other bitches, I never put them before your gold diggin' ass! You had everything and then some. If you didn't, you sure would have said something. Don't wait till a nigga fall to decide that you tired or ain't down no more!"

With tears falling from her eyes, she looked at him. "I've been down with you forever, and I always will. Whether you accept me back or not is your choice, but know that I love you. I wanna be your woman again,

more than anything in the world, and I'll do whatever it takes to get you back."

Time stood still and the silence was deafening. Monica reached for Dre and pulled him on top of her. With her legs on his shoulders, he plunged deep inside of her pussy again. Her mouth opened to speak, but no words came out. She was once again caught up in his lovemaking. It wasn't long before she finally screamed, "Dre, I'm cumming! I'm cumming! Please, don't stop!"

He watched as she grinded her pussy in circular motions on his dick. Feeling the tingling in his balls, he saw his dick go in and out of her, thickly coated with a creamy substance.

Monica grabbed Dre's thighs as she was about to cum. "Yes, yes!" she yelled, moving her head from side to side.

Dre felt her pussy pulsate around his dick, which gave him the cue that it was time for his release. "Fuuuckkkkk!" He yelled as he explored her depths while her pussy milked his dick for all it was worth.

They collapsed in the positions their bodies assumed and fell asleep.

Trying to put Deidre's mind at ease, Tony decided to rent a suite at the Sheraton. She wasn't ready to go home, or be alone, so she accepted his offer. Sitting on the couch, she rested her head in her hands.

"How you doin'?" Tony asked as he walked over to

the couch and sat next to her.

"I'm cool. It was an interesting night, that's all I can say."

"I hear ya." Tony sighed. He put his hands on her shoulders and attempted to give her a massage.

"Ummm...that feels good," Deidre said.

Tony then strategically placed his hands on pressure points to relieve some of the stress she was feeling.

"I got something else that will make you feel better," Tony replied.

Dee Dee looked at him with a quizzical expression on her face.

"I meant the Jacuzzi."

"Oh," Dee Dee said sheepishly. "Sure, that'll be fine."

Tony tested the water and turned the pressure up a little higher. He helped Dee Dee get in. The two sat, trying to rid themselves of the stress they encountered earlier. Although the atmosphere was relaxing, Dee Dee was uncomfortable being on the North Side. It was too close to where Rich lived but she didn't tell Tony of her concerns. He had already convinced her that there was nothing to worry about, and she believed him.

As Tony continued his massage, concentrating on another tense area, he spoke. "Baby, you know, I still haven't figured out how someone as beautiful and sweet as you could end up with a such a maniac. It's obvious he thinks you are indebted to him for the things he's done for you. He's not going to stop harass-

ing you until someone puts a stop to it. I wish you would let me handle this."

She knew his words were true; however, Rich would not give in easily. She was tired of the whole ordeal and just wanted to focus on something else at the moment. She purred some undistinguished comment as his hands roamed her body.

Gently gliding his hands over her breasts and down to her stomach, he hesitated. His head was telling him one thing, but his other head was saying something else.

"Don't stop," she whispered.

His hands left the resting place on her stomach and instinctively moved downward, slipping inside her bikini and gently stroking her pussy. Opening her legs to give him better access, she turned, reaching out for him. As she caressed his swollen manhood, her hand froze and eyes opened at once. *What the fuck is this?* she thought to herself. What could have been compared to a gigantic cucumber was actually Tony's dick. *Aw yeah, I hit the muthafuckin' jackpot*, she said silently to herself as she smiled at him.

Enjoying the force of the water, in addition to Tony's magical finger movements, her juices began to flow. It had been a while since she was intimate with someone, let alone a man with a dick as huge as Tony's. The thought that he was well-endowed made her bout of celibacy worth the wait.

Tony pulled her bikini to the side and attempted to enter her slowly.

"Does it hurt?" he asked when he sensed some resistance.

Deidre gasped when she felt the tip of his dick enter her. "No. Just be gentle baby, it's been a while."

Tony withdrew and re-entered her, bit by bit, until her pussy accepted him—almost all of him. He explored spots that had never been discovered before.

"Right there, baby!" she yelled.

He thrust deeper.

"Oh shit, oh shit…right there!"

Enjoying the sweet sensation her pussy gave him, he stopped in mid-stroke. Deidre looked up at Tony. "What's wrong?" she asked.

He looked at her with a menacing smile on his face. She couldn't help but smile back because she was caught up in the spell cast upon her by his magic wand.

"Come with me." He stood up and helped her out of the Jacuzzi. Picking her up, he carried her to the master bedroom to continue what they started. Laying her on the bed, Tony unceasingly made love to her. Pleased with the fact she was almost able to accommodate him, his patience and skills took her to new heights.

Turning her over on her stomach, Tony entered her from the back. Her wetness allowed him to slide deeper inside, touching places she never knew existed.

"Ooh Tony..." she said, out of breath. "I'm about to cum!"

"Go ahead baby, I wanna feel you cum," Tony grunted as he sped up his rhythm. With his deep stroke, Deidre came, and her body jerked uncontrollably.

Letting her orgasm subside, Tony pulled himself out and lay on his back. He still hadn't gotten his off. Although exhausted, Deidre climbed on top and rode him. Her pussy conformed to his girth. Just as she was about to reach another orgasm, Tony started panting then increased his speed and grabbed her hips.

"I'm cumming…I'm cumming!" he yelled as he shot his load into her vagina. The sensation lasted for what seemed like hours. After a short rest, they continued to sex each other well into the night, until the sun rose.

It was midnight when Mookie turned off 16th Avenue into the alley behind his house. He contemplated leaving the jet skis until morning, but decided against it. His neighborhood had a high crime rate, so he went ahead and tackled the task. As he started unhooking the trailer, he heard a strange sound in his garage. He paused to listen. Hearing the noise again, he spun around, reaching for his gun. He found himself looking down the barrel of Nine's automatic pistol.

"One more step and you late," Nine said, mocking Mookie's words from earlier. "Matter of fact, you late

regardless!"

Mookie couldn't believe he got caught slipping. The look in Nine's eyes told the whole story. He knew he had to do something quick. In a valiant attempt to save his life, he threw his arm up, knocking the gun out of Nine's hand. They both watched as the gun hit the floor, discharging the bullet in the chamber. Mookie reached again for the gun in the small of his back and aimed it at Nine's head. Out of the corner of the garage, Rich fired the .357 Magnum he held, aimed directly at Mookie. The sound from the large caliber pistol was deafening in the small, enclosed area and the bullet was deadly as it pierced Mookie's brain, killing him instantly.

Silence filled the garage as they both watched Mookie's body twitch on the floor until it stopped. Nine smiled as he wiped the matter of Mookie's brains from his face.

"Nine! Nine!" Rich had to call his name repeatedly before he came out of his trance.

With blood all over his shirt, he looked at his partna. "Man, I need to change this muthafucka!" Rich threw him his shirt, leaving him in a T-shirt.

They surveyed the area for evidence and stepped out into the calm of the night as though nothing had happened. They appeared poised as they made their way to the car, which was parked a short but safe distance away. Nothing about their actions revealed that they had just

taken a life. There was no regret or remorse for Mookie or anybody else who crossed the line.

Dre left Monica in the middle of the night, regretful that he'd shown weakness by fucking her. It wasn't a part of the plan that had been in place for so many years, but he charged it to the game.

Early the next morning, he called Ebony. He needed to send J-Boogie, Dollar and Killa five grand apiece. Also, he promised to see her during the upcoming weekend.

Next, he checked up on his men to see how they were coming along with the dope. To his surprise, they were already done and waiting for the next batch to be delivered. Deep down, he knew he was ahead of himself—too deep in the game too soon—but he was blinded by the half-a-million-dollar bankroll he was sitting on. For one short minute, he reflected back on the many warnings that had recently come his way—first E, then Ebony and especially last night with Monica.

When Dre turned the corner of his sister's block, he noticed a Grand Marquis in her driveway. Knowing a police car when he saw one, he kept going. He stopped at a gas station a few blocks away and called.

"What's up?" he asked.

"Someone broke into my house last night," Deidre said, irritated.

"I'm on my way."

Driving back to the house, something still didn't sit well with Dre. As he walked up the driveway, he glanced inside the car. The computer mounted to the dash and the police badge on the seat caused his heart to pound like a jackhammer. He was about to turn around again when his sister opened the door. He entered the house and looked around. The first thing he noticed was that there was no forced entry, meaning the person must have had a key. The second thing that struck him was that nothing was missing.

"Dee, how do you know someone broke in here?"

"When I got home, all of the doors were open, all of the lights were on and the stereo and TV were blasting. We didn't leave shit like that, Dre."

Looking at the person questioning her, Dre noticed he was a plain-clothes officer. *But why would he be out of uniform and on a burglary call?* Dre thought.

"Dee, is this the nigga who was at the picnic?"

"Yes, but—"

"Girl, have you lost yo' fuckin' mind!" Dre grabbed her and pulled her into the back room.

Tony heard muffled sounds, but he continued to finish his report so he could turn it in when his shift started.

Tony became uncomfortable because he knew he was the cause of Dre's anger. His plan was to drop Dee Dee off and keep going, not wanting to risk the chance

of Dre seeing his car. But he knew he couldn't because of the break-in and the fact that he liked her. He knew that once Dre found out he was a cop, it would be almost impossible to convince him he wasn't trying to bring him no shade. Truth be told, some of his closest friends were hustlers at one time or another. He had to respect Dre's frame of mind, but he wasn't going to back down.

Tony heard a door open. Deidre and Dre reappeared. Her eyes were red and Dre had anger written all over his face. Dre attempted to walk past Tony, but he stopped him. "Dre, can I holla at you for a second?"

Not wanting to overplay his hand, Dre held his composure. He hoped he wouldn't have to decide between jail and Tony's life because that was an easy choice. "What's up, *Officer?*"

"I know you're fucked up because of my status, or should I say, occupation. But meeting your sister wasn't planned, it isn't part of some kind of investigation or anything other than a lucky encounter." He smiled at Deidre. "I'm glad it happened because I'm really diggin' her, and that's my only reason for being here. I ain't concerned with any other activity. I came up out of the hood, and I respect a hustler. I ain't gonna never knock a man's hustle. Before I do that, they can have this badge."

As heartfelt as his words were, Dre couldn't allow himself to become lax around Tony. Dre clearly knew

and understood how they operated, and they were definitely untrustworthy. He had seen the police do anything to build a case, and felt this could be one of them. Dre hoped for Tony's sake that he wasn't on borrowed time because he would pull a 187 if necessary, holding court in the streets before going back to jail.

"I hear what you're saying, but I can't figure out why. You saw that shit earlier. Why would you risk your life for a piece of ass, nigga? The ends don't justify the means, partna. Because while you chasing a piece of pussy, shit gon' turn real nasty if you hurt her or if I feel the least bit nervous about you."

Tony overlooked the insult to his character. "Check this out, Dre. I respect the fact that you're on top of your game, but don't trip, especially if my position is the only thing worrying you. Shit, you gotta do what you gotta do. My mother's father was the first black Sheriff in Cook County, so I was expected to enter into Law Enforcement. I wanted to become an attorney, but my grandfather wanted me on what he considered the right side of the law. Seeing me in a uniform was his dying wish, and I became complacent like so many other officers but..." Tony hung his head. "I couldn't let him down." He looked at Dre. "Besides, you know it's been said that 'what don't hurt you can help you,' you know."

Even Tony wasn't sure what he meant by those words but one thing was for certain. He wouldn't let

anything happen to this woman because he wanted her as his own. His mind wandered and his eyes came to rest on Dee Dee.

"Man, save us all the heartache and drama. Find you someone that play fair like you do," Dre said.

"Why don't you let your sister make her own decisions?"

This struck a nerve with Dre. He understood where Officer Tony was coming from. But he knew he needed to protect his sister. They both looked at Dee Dee, and she found a spot on the floor where she fixated her gaze, never looking up at either of them.

Dre was frustrated. "Dee Dee, you need to handle your business." He left the room.

Tony watched until Dre was out of sight before turning to face her. "Well, do you have any say so in this matter?"

The clock ticking on the wall seemed magnified in the silence that followed. Exasperated, he spoke again, "So, this is where we're at, huh? You let your brother's misconception of me destroy what we have without saying a word? Yet you constantly run back to a muthafucka that's beating your ass every other day! I gave you more credit than that, Dee Dee." He reached for his cell phone that was on the table and put it in the clip.

She watched as he began to gather his stuff. Her heart fluttered at the truth and obvious disappointment in his words. She, too, felt the same pain he felt and wanted to be with him just as much as he wanted to be with her. But she thought the situation was bigger than her. The memories of the passion-filled night they shared only hours before were still fresh in her mind. Her words caught in her throat as she tried to reason with him.

"Tony, Dre is right. Don't get in over your head. I enjoyed last night and you know that I'm feeling you, but let's leave well enough alone."

They stared at each other for a moment. "An official copy of the report will be at the station. You can come by to pick it up any time. Have a good day, Miss Smith." He turned and walked out the door.

FIVE

All week Dre felt something wasn't quite right, but he couldn't put his finger on it. He thought about changing his plans to visit Ebony, but he knew it would crush her. As he approached the entrance to the highway, he called Eric. Talking to E, he was informed that no one had heard from Mookie in almost a week. When he suggested canceling his trip, Eric persuaded him to go ahead and enjoy the time off.

At two o'clock a.m., the road was empty. He wanted to get to Champaign early so that he could enjoy the entire weekend. It was the first time that he'd put the Viper full speed on the highway and was impressed with its power and stability. He stayed well over the 65 mph speed limit, activated the cruise control and fired

up a blunt. He settled in to the Isley Brothers' "*Mission to Please*" CD.

The state trooper's high beams and flashing lights lit up the inside of his car.

"Shit!" Dre yelled as the lights blinded him.

For one quick moment, he panicked as he remembered the suitcase filled with money in the back of the car. Knowing he was only speeding, he settled down and stashed the ounce of weed he carried in his crotch. He tossed the blunt then pulled over.

The officer, with a red face and his hand hovering over his gun, approached the driver's window. Dre, trying not to make any suspicious moves, let the window down.

"Good morning, sir."

Without returning his greeting, the officer spoke. "Wherever you're going young man, you seem to be in a mighty big hurry!" He overtly inspected the inside of the car. "Do you have a valid driver's license, registration and proof of insurance?"

Dre cut the interior light on, making the officer's visual search easier. He calmly got his license out of his back pocket and leaned toward the glove compartment for the officer's other request. "Here you are, sir."

"Thank you," the officer said, studying Dre's license. "Sit tight, I'm just going to call this in." The officer made his way back over to his vehicle and used his walkie-talkie to run a check on Dre.

Dre settled into the seat and adjusted the rearview mirror. A thousand scenarios played out in his head, but he opted to let the situation run its natural course.

The officer returned slightly more suspicious, aggressive and disrespectful than when he left. Having learned that Dre was recently released from prison, he set out to give him a hard time in addition to a ticket for seventeen miles over the speed limit. "Mr. Smith, before you go, I'd like to ask you a few questions."

Dre knew where this was headed and tried to cut it off beforehand. "Sir, with all due respect, I'm in a bit of a hurry and would appreciate it if you would let me be on my way. You wrote me a ticket for speeding, which I presume was your reason for stopping me."

At that moment, a backup squad car pulled up. Stepping out of the patrol car, the black officer approached both men.

"Is there a problem, Humbolt?"

"Negative, Moody. Mr. Smith was just on his way. Have a safe trip, Mr. Smith."

"Thanks," Dre said as he pulled back onto the road.

Dre covered the remaining miles to Ebony's house in less than an hour. It was 3:15 a.m. when he arrived. He decided to play a trick on her and called from the parking lot.

"Hello?" Ebony yawned as she answered the phone.

"What's happening, shorty?"

Hearing his voice, she woke instantly. "DeAndre! Hi, boo! Please tell me you're calling to say you're on you way." Ebony's excitement could be felt through the phone.

"As bad as I need to see you, I wish that was true."

"What?" Ebony's tone changed.

"It's not this weekend, but next. I hope you aren't mad at me."

The disappointment in Ebony's voice confirmed her feelings for him. "Shit! I done waited this long, I can't see how another week will kill me. I can't speak for your friend though, she's really missing you."

He laughed. "I wonder how she made it the five years I was away. I'm sure she had plenty of men to keep her company as sweet as she is."

"That's not funny, DeAndre! Besides, I've gotten pretty good at pleasing myself lately. It's less headache," she responded in a matter-of-fact tone.

Dre made it to the door and inserted the key that Ebony had given him into the lock. He continued to talk to Ebony in attempt to keep her distracted. He tiptoed inside and closed the door, still undetected.

"That sounds erotic, like something exciting to watch or listen to. Can I share in that pleasure with you?"

"If that's what you want baby, but it would be so much better if you were here with me," she said as she slid the covers off of her, easing her hand between her

legs.

He watched from the opening in her bedroom door as he listened to her on the phone.

"What are you doing right now?" he asked.

"Rubbing my pussy."

"Are you wet?"

Inserting a finger inside, " Very."

"Put two in there for me."

She eased her index and middle fingers inside of herself and slowly moved them in and out then rubbed them in a circular motion around her clitoris. "Umm...Dre, this feels good."

"Now take them out and lick your juices off."

She obeyed.

"Dre, I'm imagining your dick sliding inside me right now. Can you imagine that?"

"Fo' sho', I can," he said. He was ready to walk into the room. His dick was straining against his pants and needed to be released, but he stayed on the other side of the door a minute longer.

Her voice trembled and her breathing became erratic as he continued talking. Her climax approached fast. He wished his penis was inside of her juicy vagina as he watched her masturbate.

"Oh, baby. I'm about to cum," she whispered into the phone.

"Cum for me, baby. You know I love to hear you when you cum."

Just as she moaned in satisfaction, he stepped inside the room in plain view. The sight of him caused another orgasm to wash over her.

"You gonna just stand there and look, or do you want to participate?" she asked, smiling at him as she continued to stroke herself.

As he made his way over to the bed, she stared at him. "You are so wrong, Mr. Smith, but I still love you. That was such a dirty game but I enjoyed it," she whispered as she opened her legs wider for him to get a good look at her juices as they coated the inside of her thighs.

He undressed and eased into bed with her. "I think I got the most enjoyment out of that," he said, lying beside her.

They made intense and passionate love until the sun came up. As always, their love was never dictated by their time apart. The moments they were together mattered the most. The best thing was, when they were together, Dre left all of his problems at the door.

The day was filled with shopping, a matinee, lunch and an intimate walk in the park. After playing on the swings like two people in love, they eventually settled on one of the benches. Cuddled up, they brought each other abreast of the happenings in their lives. Dre told Ebony about Mookie's absence, Dee Dee's dilemma and his uncertainty with Monica as well as his appreciation for her and the serenity she brought into his life.

She touched on the little things she wanted from him, but as always, she listened, choosing to let him decide how important she was to him, and how their relationship would proceed. Regardless of her feelings for him, she always tried to keep him thinking and planning. Not paying attention to the time, it was well into the night when they arrived back at her place.

The weekend passed too quickly. Dre found himself sitting on the side of the bed late Sunday night, regretting having to leave. He enjoyed being with Ebony and she relished his company as well. He looked over at her as she lay naked beside him, still sexually sedated from their evening of lovemaking. He stroked her cheek.

He walked over to the package he had on Ebony's dresser and sealed it. It was ready to be sent to his workers via FedEx. As he counted the stacks of money he laid out on the dresser, Ebony began to stir.

"Hey baby," she said quietly as she stretched.

"Hey sleepy head." Continuing to count the money, he asked, "How much do you need, baby?"

"I don't need anything but you, daddy."

Walking toward the bed, he was aroused by her tone. He placed a bundle of cash, already counted, on her nightstand and climbed in beside her.

He placed kisses over her entire body before he settled at his intended destination. He inhaled the sweet aroma of her sex and with all inhibitions aside, parted the folds of her labia with his tongue. He took his time as he made love to her. Before they were through, no part of her queen-sized bed was left untouched.

◆ ◆ ◆

Police cars were everywhere. Homicide investigators roped off access to the murder scene with yellow tape. The neighborhood had an eerie feeling and the smell of death hung next to Mookie's house. Trying to gather what happened, E sat on the back porch and stared into the early morning sky. The pain of his partna's death was etched onto his face as he tried to re-enact the murder and how Mookie was caught off guard. The police couldn't uncover a motive, but in E's mind, there was no question about who was responsible for this tragedy.

The paramedics exiting the garage brought him out of his musings. He covered the distance to the stretcher where the body lay. The body bag that housed Mookie seemed to be calling Eric. Wanting to be certain, he unzipped the bag. He was taken aback by the sight before him—Mookie's decomposing body with maggots feasting on the hole where the bullet pierced his brain. As tears ran down his cheeks, E reached to close what was left of Mookie's eyes. *Bastards couldn't even close his eyes*, E thought to himself. The paramedics loaded the corpse into the ambulance and pulled off.

E spoke to the fading body, "The nigga that did this is gonna pay, believe that, homie!"

The wails from Dee Dee, Trina, Monica and Mya

were heart-wrenching as they stood off to the side, trying to console one another. They knew this was just the beginning of the bloodshed.

Any feelings Dee Dee might have had left for Rich were gone. She knew that the body being carried away could've easily been hers, Dre's or any of the others'. She couldn't help but feel that she was the cause of Mookie's death.

After the police, paramedics and investigators left, everyone went inside to await the arrival of Mookie's family from Milwaukee.

Tony sat in his squad car a short distance away, but was in sight of Mookie's house. He hoped to get a glimpse of Dee Dee. A week had passed since he last saw her and he felt as though his world was crumbling. No matter how hard he tried, he couldn't shake his thoughts of being with her. He still recalled the last words she spoke to him. *Leave well enough alone*, she said. By what had just transpired, it was obvious that she knew what she was talking about.

When he had heard the dispatcher's call, summoning all available units, he knew something was wrong. The address sounded familiar. It dawned on him that this was because he ran a check on everyone after the incident at the picnic. He was relieved when he arrived and learned that Dee Dee was all right. The thought of something happening to her was paralyzing. He reached for his phone and dialed her number but hung up before she could answer.

Everyone went into the den. Behind the bar, Trina poured for everyone. They sipped from their glasses. Choosing to keep their thoughts private, no one spoke. Lil Greg, a close friend from Cleveland, arrived a short time later with his woman, Cassandra.

Trina, being the perfect hostess, made sure everyone had what they needed.

"Has anyone called to tell Dre what happened?" Lil Greg inquired.

"Yeah, I called him," Monica responded. "He said he was a couple of hours away and would be here as soon as possible." She hid her anger knowing that Dre was in Champaign with Ebony. He didn't try to hide that fact from her.

"Eric, who found him?" Cassandra asked, trying not to break down and cry. It was no use as the tears rolled down her face.

"His neighbor found him this morning as he was leaving for work. He told the police that after not seeing him for a week or so, he decided to check his garage. That's when he spotted him lying on the ground, dead."

Dee Dee could take no more, so she went into the living room to wait for Mookie's mother, Mrs. Campbell, to arrive. There were so many thoughts run-

ning through her mind that she felt like she was going insane. She was momentarily distracted by the squad car passing the house. For a split second, she thought she recognized Tony as the driver but thought better of it. Contemplating the retrieval of her ringing cell phone, the arrival of Mrs. Campbell and the rest of Mookie's family changed her mind. *Whoever it was will call back if it's important*, she said to herself.

"Mrs. Campbell just arrived," Dee Dee informed the crew as she walked back into the den.

E stood and addressed everyone in the house. "Check this out, let's not make matters worse for her by revealing our suspicions. We don't want her, or anybody else, to tip the police to the perpetrators. It's street justice on this one, fo' sho'!"

It proved difficult trying to hide the facts from Mrs. Campbell, but they managed. She took grieving to a whole new level as she fell out on the floor, asking God *why*. Her daughter, Shay, was right by her side.

E, along with Mookie's two brothers, Lucky and A.D., went outside to talk privately. E didn't want to deny them knowledge of what actually happened. As E explained, to the best of his ability, Dre came to a screeching halt in the alley.

Dre was furious as he sat in a trance, listening. He felt like Rich should have dealt with him instead of someone who didn't have anything to do with it. The beef was with Dre, not Mookie. They all sat huddled together, devising a plan of revenge that would bar none.

Their conversation was cut short when Mrs. Campbell came outside in search of her sons. It was time to go to the morgue. She needed them with her when she identified Mookie's body, a task she wasn't sure she could accomplish alone. Her eyes were puffy and she looked like she hadn't slept in weeks. The death of her son, worry and the financial strains of a funeral aged her about ten years in a matter of minutes.

Dre reassured Mrs. Campbell that he would take care of the funeral expenses. It was the least he could do. She pulled him into her arms, assuring him that she didn't blame him and that she appreciated him and Eric for all they had done.

Not far from the gathering in Maywood, Rich and Nine were packing their bags as they watched a breaking news bulletin on television.

The police are at the scene of what appears to be a homicide in the Maywood area. There are no suspects at this time and the name of the victim is not being released until family is notified. We will bring you more on this situation as we receive new information. Now back to your regularly scheduled programming.

Even after hearing that there were no suspects, they were still uneasy. They knew that a war had been started so they decided to take a long overdue vacation.

"Yeah! They can add that one to another episode of

unsolved mysteries," Rich spat as he shoved a heap of cocaine up his nose. A photo of Dee Dee sat on the table next to the drugs. "That bitch and her brother don't realize who they fuckin' with. That nigga talking 'bout, 'one more step and you late.' Who late now? Seems like it's him, 'cause that nigga been dead for damn near two weeks." His laugh was menacing and terrifying. "That sounds like closed casket action to me!"

Their blatant disregard for a life was tangible. Since they were old enough to carry a pistol, they lived according to "the kill or be killed" mentality. The repercussions of their actions were never added into the equation, because they had never suffered in the past. They grabbed their bags, secured the house and headed toward the airport to catch their flight.

SIX

The building that Dre purchased for Dee Dee's beauty salon was located east on 87th Street, between Jeffrey and Stoney Island Avenue. Although it wasn't furnished, it was spacious enough to comfortably accept the many that were to meet there to discuss the plans regarding the avenging of Mookie's death. About a dozen of them had combed the West Side streets of Chi Town, the area where most of Rich's drug activity went down and where a few of his stash houses were believed to be. They hoped to catch up with him or Nine.

The locations Dee Dee gave them proved to be accurate but they didn't want to act prematurely by raiding the spots and smashing Rich's crew. After having no luck in their search, they returned to the meeting place.

They decided to save their surprise until after the funeral. The wee hours of the night found them all sitting around, drinking and smoking while reminiscing about Mookie and old times.

The arrangements for the funeral were handled smoothly and quickly. No one wanted to prolong the inevitable. Everyone was as prepared as they could be for the solemn days ahead. Dre's bankroll had grown immensely. He and Eric made sure their partna's celebration spared no expense.

All of the out-of-town relatives and friends were in Chicago a day or two prior to the funeral. Ebony came as well, and Dre spent the night before the service with her at the Downtown Continental Hotel.

The home-going procession cast a cloud of gloom over the entire 82nd block of Jeffrey. The presence of the many police cars directing traffic acted as a sort of wall, cutting the procession off from the violence that could erupt at any given moment. Dre didn't expect anything to jump off; he wanted Mrs. Campbell's mind at ease. It put E's mind to rest as well because it was next to impossible to recognize the many people behind the heavily tinted windows of all the unfamiliar cars.

There were six limousines. The immediate family occupied the first three, while distant relatives and close friends were in two and the crew—Dre and Ebony, E and Trina, Lil Greg and Cassandra and Dee Dee—were

in the very last limo. Dre was in his own world as he stared blankly at the passing scenery. When he glanced at E with Trina snuggled up under him, he thought back to the night of his party and the Fourth of July picnic. He shook his head at how conniving and deceptive women were. However, that seemed to be the least of his partna's worries. He eventually shook the thought out of his head because he knew E's game was airtight. Dee Dee sat next to Trina, and it had not gone unnoticed that she was the only one without a companion. There was a glimmer of loneliness in her eyes. Dre wished he could soothe his sister's soul, wished that she could find someone who would make her happy and treat her like a lady. He loved Dee Dee and refused to watch her throw her life away with a bitch-ass nigga like Rich or with some cop who's probably trying to spin her. Then, he realized his arm was protectively around Ebony. At that moment, he knew she was his missing rib—the woman he wanted to always be by his side.

The limos came to rest in front of Calvary Baptist Church. The first person he saw as he exited the car was Monica, walking past them with a female friend. Dre nodded at her as he extended his hand to assist the women out of the car.

Everyone took a brief moment to make sure they were on point. All were dressed to the nines. The men were in dark suits, tailored to fit as alligator shoes donned their feet. Ebony wore a navy blue Jones New

York linen pencil skirt and jacket with a pair of sling-back pumps, while Dee Dee, Trina and Cassandra wore sexy, yet conservative, designer dresses with the stilettos and purse to match. Dee Dee and Dre must have spotted Tony at the same time, because they both looked as they tried to gauge the other's reaction. As if reading each other's mind, they glanced around to see if anyone else had recognized Tony. No one had. Turning back to his sister, Dre wondered if she had anything to do with his presence. His curiosity remained as one of the assistant funeral directors came to lead them into the church.

The sounds of the organ could be heard from the stairway. As they were ushered into the sanctuary, the sight of the white oak casket forced everyone into the difficult and unwanted task before them. An array of flowers, from Carnations to Birds of Paradise, surrounded it. There were so many flowers that you would have thought you were attending a beloved Italian mobster's service.

Once seated, all the lights dimmed except those that shone down upon the casket with platinum handles that had Mookie's initials engraved into them. A large screen slowly descended from the ceiling. A portrait of Mookie claimed everyone's attention. Shay, through constant tears, narrated the various clips of her brother's life. It appeared that every year of Mookie's existence had been documented. All the birthdays, holidays, picnics and vacations were caught on video. There were a few people taking the unexpected twist of fate very hard, but for the most part, everyone held up pretty well or as well as could be expected. Then came the pictures of all of them, which included Dre and Dee Dee's parents at their family reunion. That one moment in Mookie's life brought the entire room to tears. Dre and Mookie were young teenagers, dressed in cut-off jeans, no shirt and PRO-Keds with nappy hair. A groan escaped Dre's throat, not only for his partna, but also for him and his sister. That was the last time they saw their parents alive. Later that night, after a heated argument, their father fatally shot their mother and then himself due to wrongful accusations of infidelity.

Dre created a chain reaction, and before long the entire room filled with wails and screams. The more current pictures of Mookie's life seemed to take a toll on everyone, so the funeral directors decided to stop the video.

Dee Dee's eyes were filled with tears, but her face was expressionless, as though her mind was preoccupied with distant thoughts. Dre watched her get up and leave, having a good idea where she was going. Remembering her state of loneliness in the limo, he left it alone.

Ebony felt Monica's eyes boring into her, and the hatred in them was obvious. She hoped Monica was woman enough to accept Dre's choice but wasn't

intimidated by her at all. After a long bout of staring, Ebony decided to get up and get a drink of water. She needed some fresh air.

"Baby, I'll be right back." She smiled, giving Dre a quick peck on the cheek.

"Aight, hurry back."

"I will."

With a wicked grin on her face, Monica watched as Ebony sashayed out the room. *That bitch think she the shit*, she thought as she chuckled and shook her head. *Well I got something for you, hoe.* Tired of Ebony's presence in her man's life, Monica got up as well. In her mind the bitch had to go and that day would be good enough as any to get rid of her. Out of the corner of his eye Dre could see Monica making her move. He knew the chick had chicken head tendencies, but did she have to start an argument at his man's funeral? Deciding he needed to set things straight between them once and for all, Dre got up too and followed her outside.

It was several minutes before Dee Dee found Tony standing in the shade of a large tree. Even then, she hesitated because she didn't know what to say or how he would react. He saw her approaching but kept his gaze diverted to avoid showing his anxiety.

"Hey." She walked closer. "I hope I'm not disturbing you. Do you have a minute?"

He lifted his head without looking directly at her.

"Well, you know aiding and assisting is part of my job. What's happening, Miss Smith?" He finally looked at her. *Damn she look good*, he thought.

"I'm surprised to see you here," she said, looking at him. *Damn, he looks good in that uniform*, her mind roamed.

"What, you want me to leave?" Tony asked sarcastically.

She smiled at his sarcasm. "No. I'm glad you're here. It's good seeing you again." She waited until their eyes met before continuing. "Tony, I'm sorry for the way things went down between us."

"You could have fooled the shit out of me!"

"You know it wasn't because I ain't feeling you. You know that, Tony. It was just the opposite." She stepped into his line of vision. "And for whatever it's worth, I miss you." She reached out and touched his hand.

He took a moment to gather his thoughts. "Dee Dee, when I first met you, I was instantly attracted to you, even under the circumstances. After getting to know you, I have a lot of respect for you. I can see why your brother said what he said but I figured, at some point, both of you would see me for what I am, a nigga that struggles every day just like ya'll. I would never wish or cause you any harm."

Dee Dee looked away, trying to hold back the tears forming in her eyes.

"I don't know about the previous cats in your life, but when I care for someone, I don't want to see noth-

ing happen to them that don't happen to me first. I hope you don't miss your blessing because you're scared to try something new."

Unable to suppress the tears that welled in her eyes, she let them fall freely. "I won't. That's why I'm here now. I don't care what anyone else thinks. I'm just trusting that you want to be a part of my life for the reason you say you do and nothing more." She paused for a second then continued. "Nobody has put me first without hurting me, so, of course, I will be skeptical. I'm willing to give you a chance but I can't afford to be hurt again. If this isn't something you can do, let me walk away and forget we ever had this conversation."

Dre stood in the hallway staring out of the window unnoticed. Their focus was on each other. Even the funeral in progress was temporarily forgotten. Dee Dee and Tony felt this was their last chance to reveal everything their hearts held inside. "Can I ask you a question, Dee?"

"Yes."

"Have you seen or heard from Rich lately?"

"No, I haven't, and I ain't trying to hear from that nigga, either. You can see what he's been up to," she said, waving her arm at the church, cars and all the people. "I know he's responsible for this. Tony, this was my one and only reason for not wanting you around. I'm too dangerous to be around. This is serious."

"It's amazing that you are so concerned about me,

someone who can hold his own yet be so reckless with your own safety. I know you came to tell me something better than that."

She moved closer toward him. Standing up on her toes, she placed a juicy kiss upon his lips. "That's what I came to say. Did you hear me?" She smiled.

"Yeah, I hear you, but I don't understand what you're saying."

"I'm saying that things can be different if you still want them to be."

"By all means, baby," he responded then kissed her long and passionately, finding himself not really caring who saw them. He could be reprimanded because it was against the Chicago Police Department's policy to openly show public displays of affection while on duty, but it didn't even faze him. He would do whatever he had to do to keep her.

Still looking, Dre became angry that Tony and Dee were showing disregard for his disapproval for their relationship; however, he knew she deserved to be happy. *He really must like her or he's just a stupid-ass nigga waiting to die*, he thought as he looked back at the church, knowing what Rich was capable of doing. He turned to gaze out of the window at Dee Dee and Tony. He knew Tony deserved a chance and accepted his presence as genuine.

Thinking back to the incident at Dee Dee's house, he recalled the words Tony spoke:

I respect the fact that you're on top of your game, but don't trip, especially if my position is the only thing that is worrying you. Shit, you gotta do what you gotta do. Besides, you know it's been said that 'what don't hurt you can help you,' you know.

He made a mental note to sit down and speak with Tony. *He may just come in handy*, he thought to himself as he turned and walked away to find Ebony and Monica.

♦ ♦ ♦

"Uhmm, excuse me, but can I talk to you for a second?" Monica said, tapping Ebony on the shoulder.

Knowing that Monica had some shit she needed to get off her chest, Ebony replied, "Sure."

"Look, Evonne, Elaine or whatever your damn name is," Monica spat harshly. She knew her name but didn't want to acknowledge it. "I'ma keep this short and sweet. I don't know who you are or where you came from, but I have put too much time and effort into my relationship with Dre to let some chick like you destroy, overnight, what took years for us to build. So let me give you some advice. Why don't you go 'head about your business and find some other nigga to latch on to, 'cause Dre is mine."

Ebony's eyes rolled back in her head as she clenched and unclenched her fist. Her first instinct was to knock the shit out of Monica, but she didn't want to stoop to her level or cause a scene at Mookie's funeral. Still, she wasn't going to back down or bite her tongue.

"Relationship?" Ebony laughed. "You destroyed

your *relationship* when you left him high and dry, but I guess considering the kind of gold diggin' bitch you are, that's just how you get down. I guess you thought you could ease your way back in when he got home, but guess what, he don't want your skank ass. He wants me, and by the way, you know my name, bitch."

Monica was in awe at Ebony's words but didn't let that stop her from saying what she had to say. "That little speech was cute, but you see, what's so sad about it is that you don't have a clue. 'Cause if Dre didn't want me, he wouldn't have been laid up in my bed the other night!" Monica smiled as though she had revealed a top secret piece of information.

"So, you think I give a fuck? Dre don't give a fuck about you, hoe! All he wanted to do was get his dick wet and yo' dumb ass let him!" Ebony spat, pissed. Realizing that she was letting Monica get to her, Ebony toned it down. "You know what? I ain't got time for this. Yo' wack ass ain't even worth it. You's a lil' girl with a lil' girl's mentality, and I am too much of a fuckin' woman to deal with this bullshit. So let me break it down like this for you, boo boo. If Dre want to be wit' you...he can be wit' you. I'ma be cool regardless. 'Cause I will be damned if I run in behind him like you, stalking and sniffing up his ass, begging, like some desperate stupid bitch!"

Ebony's words hit home and Monica felt herself losing it. Raising her fist in the air she was just about to

strike Ebony when Dre busted through the doors.

"What the fuck is going on out here? Ya'll lost ya'll fuckin' mind?" he yelled, grabbing Monica's arm before it could land on Ebony's face.

Ebony spoke up. "Just this crazy bitch, steady eye-fucking me everywhere I go like she got a problem or something!"

"You damn right I got a problem! I'm sick and tired of this bitch being in the way!" Monica wanted to retract her words but it was too late.

"In the way? In the way of what, Mo?"

"Us! That's what!"

"Us? There ain't no us!" Dre was getting fed up with this same redundant conversation.

"But—"

"Mo, I told you before, Ebony is my woman. I don't want you, and you know that," Dre interrupted.

Monica was on the verge of screaming. "Your woman, huh? What kind of bullshit is that? She wasn't your woman when you was fuckin' me the other night!"

Unable to defend himself, Dre stood silent.

"Oh don't get quiet, nigga! Tell yo' so-called woman how you fucked me not once but twice!"

Dre looked at Ebony, unable to read her expression, then looked back at Monica. She had a smirk on her face as if she had conquered the world. *Damn, I gotta think of something quick*, he panicked.

Dre turned his nose up as if a foul stench was in the air. "Man please get the fuck outta here. Don' t nobody want yo' skank ass. Like I told you before, I'm through fuckin' wit you so get that through yo' loony-ass brain." Monica's mouth dropped. As he held out his hand for Ebony, she proudly accepted it and before they walked away, he continued. "Now if you'll excuse us, we need to finish paying our respects." Walking past, Ebony smiled as she held Monica's stare in the palm of her hands.

She watched as they reentered the chapel. "You'll get yours, muthafucka! Watch!" she hissed underneath her breath as the door closed.

The service, although emotional, went without a hitch. Everyone met at Mookie's house for the repast. They ate, drank and celebrated just as Mookie would have wanted. Everybody was present, except Monica. Throughout the entire repast Dre could tell that Ebony was upset even though she tried to deny it. She knew deep in her heart that Monica's words were true, but what could she do, Dre wasn't her man. Their relationship hadn't even been considered official until that day.

Dre looked in her direction as he held a conversation wit' his boys. Ebony was seated on the couch with her legs crossed gazing out the window. She looked so sad. The thought of her hurting because of him tore Dre up inside but what could he say, *I fucked up?* That shit wouldn't fly, and besides, Ebony deserved more than that.

Deciding that something needed to be said, he walked over to the couch and took a seat beside her.

"Penny for your thoughts."

"They cost more than that," she replied, giving him a half-hearted smile.

"Yo, we need to talk."

"Look...you don't owe me any explanations. I'm not your chick. I'm just a person you kick it wit' from time to time."

"But see, that's the point." He looked deep into her eyes. "I don't want you to just be a person I kick it wit' from time to time. I want you to be my girl. The one I can call all my own."

"What about Monica?"

"What about her?"

"C'mon Dre, be real wit me. I know you fucked her."

"Look, I'ma put it to you like this. A nigga got caught up in old feelings and fucked up, plain and simple."

"Thank you. It's fucked up, but thank you."

"Like, for real though, I'm feelin' you. And at first I was confused about where I wanted things to go between us. But now I know that I want you by my side. Not Monica or no other chick—you. I want you."

"I don't know, Dre. I mean that sounds good and everything but what's gonna happen when I'm the one left with a broken heart? I done been down that road before and I ain't tryin' to go back," Ebony spoke as her bottom lip began to quiver.

"Who said anything about breakin' hearts? I'm tryin' to win your heart, and when I play, I play for keeps, ma, so let's not worry about the bad stuff that comes along with being in a relationship and concentrate on us being together. I need you, girl. Don't leave me now." He kissed her lips and hugged her tight.

"I need you, too, Dre." Ebony cried. "I need you, too."

SEVEN

Fall arrived quickly in Chicago, and with it came a brisk and chilly breeze like only the Windy City could bring. Two months had passed since Mookie's death and there was still no sign of Rich or Nine. Although, word on the street was that they had taken an extended vacation out of the country.

Dre and E had just hung up the phone with Lucky and A.D. Whereas the murder was a fading memory to some, Mookie's death was still fresh and painful to his brothers and his partnas. Vengeance was still their top priority.

E's wise investments enabled him to leave the drug game alone and watch his multi-million dollar portfolio grow effortlessly. Dre had flipped six kilos of heroin

and Eric stressed to his protégé the importance of staying two steps ahead of the game. Before they could put their plan into action, they needed to be on the same page. For some reason, he felt like Dre wanted to sell dope forever.

"All that shit can wait," E said. His voice resonated throughout the expanse of the maple-paneled study. "Sometimes you scare me, homie. You need to forget about all this high-risk hustling and some low-end-ass beauty salon. That shit can wait. When we pull this thing off we'll have enough money to buy a goddamn island! You should be focused on finding somewhere to lay your head when this shit gets deep. Somewhere unknown."

Dre stood in the window, unenthused with the way E was chastising him, although he knew his words were true. "You give that nigga too much credit. That nigga ain't trying to bump heads with me," he said as he sat at the mahogany table across from E. "That's why he's hiding."

The mere seconds of silence that followed allowed Dre to predict his partna's next words. Before he could repeal his comment, E spoke.

"Main man, I know you got the heart of a lion, no doubt, but you also got tunnel vision right now. The smartest man is gonna come out on top, not the strongest. Try to look past brawn and that lil' six-month-old bankroll you sitting on. Try to see further

than tomorrow, next month or next year. Remember that just because you are eating good and got a couple broads sucking your dick, you ain't Superman and Rich ain't either."

"That's why the nigga hiding. I doubt if we'll find him standing on the strip waiting for us to blow his muthafuckin' brains out cause that's what's gonna happen when we find him."

The tension in the room was thick. Dre was submerged in his feelings by the insult of the "little" six-month-old bankroll Eric mentioned. He had two and a half million dollars stashed away, and for a minute, he wanted to inform E of that fact. Not to mention that *his* broad was offering to suck Dre's dick, too. But that was just a passing thought, as well as a pleasure, in which he would never partake. He knew his partna's words were love.

"So, what do you suggest I do?" Dre asked earnestly.

"Put your money into something that's gonna retain its value and yield a profitable return. Not no damn salon where the whole fucking world will know how to touch you." He paused for a second. "Where you keeping your cash at? Dee's house or in the ground somewhere?" E asked, laughing for the first time.

"Nah, it's safe though."

"Oh, don't tell me, Ebony's house? Seriously, get you and your loved ones out of harm's way before we put

the squeeze on this nigga, feel me?"

"Yeah, I feel you. What about you? It's not like you're burrowed forty feet under ground."

"You right. That's why I invested in this reinforced crib and state-of-the-art security system. A muthafucka can't turn on this block without being seen. And let's not forget I got some Waco type shit in the safe house."

Their conversation was cut short as the motion sensors went off and the monitors showed Trina pulling up in a brand new Jaguar XJ.

"Damn! You got Ma riding lovely. What's really good, homie? You fucked up in love or what?"

"Man, please," E retorted.

"Aw shit," Dre said as he cupped his hand over his mouth. "You thinking 'bout marrying her!"

Eric cut him a look.

"When's the wedding?" Dre was beside himself with laugher, knowing Eric wasn't going out like that.

He could sense Dre's ridicule and chose his words carefully. "Best believe that when I put a ring on a bitch's finger, she's tried and true. Trina has failed the wifey test a thousand times. I know she's slick, but at the same time, she serves a purpose." E thought back to Dre's welcome home party. He had reviewed the security camera tapes and witnessed more of what he already knew about Trina. She was a bonafide freak who wouldn't hesitate to flaunt her sex appeal behind his back. "I wouldn't be surprised if she hasn't tried to give

you some ass, but don't trip, 'cause I ain't."

They stopped talking as Trina entered the room. She wore a soft, brown suede jumpsuit that hugged every curve of her body. Placing her bags on the sofa, she handed E a large manila envelope. "What's up, fellas?" Dre nodded his head.

"Did you handle that business for me?" E asked as his eyes penetrated her mind.

"Yes. I closed the accounts and made the transfers just like you said, baby. All the paperwork is in there," Trina answered with confidence. She looked at them both and sensed by the silence she encountered when she arrived that she was the topic of conversation.

E looked over the contents of the envelope, satisfied. Her deeds had already been validated and confirmed with an earlier phone call.

Dee Dee swayed to her favorite song, playing on the radio, "*Nobody's Supposed to Be Here,*" by Deborah Cox. She was in a good mood. She and Tony had become inseparable, and best of all, he and Dre got along well. She proved wrong the saying, "absence makes the heart grow fonder," because she could have cared less about Rich. She was wide open with Tony's romantic and caring ways. Thinking of the night they had planned, she could hardly contain her excitement and couldn't wait to get off work. She put the finishing touches on Mya's hair and turned her around toward the mirror.

"All right bitch, it's a wrap."

"Damn! Don't I look good!" Mya said as she admired her new hairstyle. Dee Dee wasn't the best stylist in the city, but she was her friend. Jokingly, Dee turned up her nose and shook her head. "Don't hate me 'cause I'm beautiful, hoe," Mya said laughing, catching Dee in the act.

Mya smiled at her best friend and her choice of words. Whereas Dee Dee's outlook on life was rapidly changing—she was enjoying the peace, tranquility and normalcy of a quiet existence—Mya's wasn't. She was still obsessed with being on top of the latest fashion, newest slang and the nigga with the fattest pockets.

Her smile vanished when Dee said, "Naw, don't hate me 'cause you owe me sixty-five dollars."

"I knew it was too good to be true. Your ass up in here singing and dancing and shit. Drowning my ears with that 'I think I'm in love' shit. Then, you want to tax a playa. Bitch, please! I wish I would."

Mya grabbed her purse and headed toward the door. She turned, facing Dee Dee and smiled.

"You owe me, heifer."

Reaching toward the door, she stopped and blew her girl a kiss. "Love you. Ciao." Mya left out of the shop on a mission.

Dee smiled and shook her head as she watched the lights of Mya's new Saab convertible flash, signaling that the alarm was deactivated. "That girl can't be broke

driving that car," she mumbled to herself as she cut off the outside lights of the shop and drew the blinds. She made a mental note of all the things she'd do differently with her salon in the future.

Tony was picking her up at nine o'clock, so she brought her clothes to work with her. She picked up her trusty .380 pistol and went into the back to shower.

Thirty minutes later she was in her panties and bra, retouching her hair and applying makeup. She didn't want to miss a second of the Jagged Edge concert at the Rosemont Horizon. She hummed their song, "*Promise*," as she thought about what could be forthcoming later that night.

Ring...Ring...

Her cell phone broke her concentration. She thought it was Tony so she pressed the talk button. "Hello? Hello!" Just as she was about to hang up, an operator interrupted the silence.

"This is an international call. Please hold while you are connected."

Who could be calling me from out of the country? she thought to herself as she put on her clothes and curiously waited for the caller.

"What's up, babygirl? Hearing his voice erased all doubt, and she dropped the phone. Chill bumps covered her body. She was paralyzed. Finally, with trembling hands, she reached for the phone.

"Hello?"

Rich's voice blared through the line. "What's hap'n, stranger? Long time no hear from."

"What do you want, Rich? And why are you calling me?" Dee asked, visibly shaken.

"I was hoping that you would accept my offer of us spending some time together. Perhaps a nice vacation," he inquired in one of his sweetest baritone voices. "You know a nigga been dying to taste that sweet, juicy pussy of yours." His shot at humor was disgusting, and she cringed from the thoughts of his hands upon her body.

"Thanks, but no thanks. Do you seriously think that I would have anything to do with you after what you did?"

"Look, Dee, I'm sorry for the way I treated you, baby. I miss you." He had the game down pat, having used those lines too many times before. "Let me make it up to you." Ignoring her insinuations, he was smart not to incriminate himself.

Dee closed her eyes and took a deep breath. She hated that he still stirred something inside of her. She knew she had to say something and wash her hands of him.

"Rich, it's over. Ain't no making up, forgiving or nothing else. Please! Just go ahead on."

Exploding through the phone, he barked, "Bitch, look, I'm tired of playing this game with you! You'll see me again. That much, I promise." His voice lowered to a deep, low growl. "Don't make me resort to drastic

measures. Do you understand what I'm saying?"

She slammed the phone closed and sat back in the chair. "Why can't he leave me the fuck alone!"

Ring...Ring...

The shop phone rang. Instead of looking at the caller ID, she ran outside and saw Tony waiting for her.

The minute he saw her, he knew something was wrong. She looked like she had seen a ghost.

"Hey baby, what's up?" he greeted her as he held the passenger door open.

"Just glad to see you," she responded as she got into the car.

"Did Rich contact you?"

Not wanting to ruin their night, Dee Dee decided not to reply.

Tony knew it would take her a minute to understand that he had no ulterior motives when it came to their relationship. He drove off without pressuring her about what was going on in her mind. He figured she would talk about it when she was ready. Dee was glad to be in Tony's presence, where she felt safe. But neither of them saw the person in the car, parked in a dark cut, a short distance away.

EIGHT

Ebony was tired and her feet were sore from being on them all day. Dealing with the different attitudes and demands of the customers left her with a raging migraine. There was an unusual amount of horny men, both young and old, trying to hit on her. When the plane touched down in Chicago, she gathered her stuff in a hurry. She hadn't seen Dre in three weeks and was excited about spending the next four days with him. She was also anxious to know about the surprise he wanted to show her. Whatever it was, it was expensive because she was carrying close to a million dollars in a briefcase. Like clockwork, Dre was the first person she saw as she stepped out of the airport.

"Baby!" She ran into his arms and kissed him. She

handed him the briefcase as she leaned into his embrace.

"What's up, sexy? How was your flight?"

"Exhausting and aggravating as hell, but now it's all worth it. You know I be needing you, Mr. Smith."

Knowing what her needs were turned him on but there were other, more important matters to handle. On their way into the city, they stopped to see Mr. Mallory, a broker and personal friend of Eric's, at his office. Once the legal documents were in order, and the check was issued, he had to meet the realtor for the closing on his new home. There were a lot of strings being pulled, enabling him to purchase such an expensive crib. All the particulars reiterated the shadiness of the deal. For instance, the deed was in his deceased parents' name.

Dre had taken the conversation with Eric to heart. He realized the dangers ahead of them, and he knew he didn't want to risk someone else getting hurt or killed, especially Ebony or Dee Dee. As he pulled onto the circular, cobblestone driveway, he brought his vehicle to rest under the granite veranda, which would lead them to the eight foot double doors of his new home.

It hadn't dawned on Ebony that a new house was the surprise until the moment she laid her eyes on it. She looked at him, her exhaustion suddenly forgotten, with a face full of excitement.

"Oh Dre! I know this isn't what I think it is! Whose house is this?"

He looked at her and smiled. It was his first in a long time. Lately, there hadn't been a lot to smile about, but her happiness, as well as his own, produced a wide grin.

"Baby girl, this is ours," he answered, opening her door and wrapping her in his arms.

They were so caught up in each other that they never saw the realtor as she exited the house. She cleared her throat.

"Excuse me, Mr. Smith."

They both turned around, surprised by her standing so close to them.

"Yes," Dre answered. "Mrs. Robinson, I presume?"

"Yes. I'll be handling the closing process of your lovely home. May I ask who this beautiful young lady is?" she asked, piqued by the proud glare in his eyes.

"Please excuse me. This is my fiancée. The soon-to-be Mrs. Ebony Smith." Dre spoke with assurance. It took everything Ebony had to contain her excitement at this revelation.

"Well hello, and congratulations," the realtor said, extending her hand. "In that case, let me first show the lady of the house the exquisite kitchen in this beautiful sixty-five hundred square foot haven. I know you'll love this. It's amazing."

Two hours passed before they covered the entire house. Dre released a sigh of relief when Mrs. Robinson left. Exhausted, they sat on the floor, admiring the

thick, cottony feel of the living room carpet while enjoying the fireplace. After some time, he went into the kitchen and returned with two glasses and a bottle of Cristal. With his head resting in her lap, they stared into the flame of the fire and toasted each other.

"To a new beginning," he said.

"A new beginning," Ebony echoed.

"Oh, before I forget," he said as he passed Ebony a small, perfectly wrapped box. With tears in her eyes Ebony opened it. She was amazed to find a flawless ten-carat princess cut engagement ring designed by Jacob the Jeweler himself.

"I know I kind of asked already, but will you marry me?"

"Yes," she said, barely audible, in between tears.

Dre placed the diamond ring on the designated finger, held her hands together and kissed them.

"I can't believe this is happening," she gushed.

"I don't see why? I told you you was my girl."

"I know, it's just that everything's moving so fast. First it was the house and now this," she said, gazing down at her ring.

"Give me a kiss."

Ebony kissed him slowly and passionately.

"I love you and as long as you hold a nigga down I got you, so don't trip."

Hours passed and they were still in each other's arms. Reaching into his pocket, he found a bag a weed.

Dre busted down an Optimo and rolled a burner.

"You want some?" he asked.

"Nah, I'm straight."

Dre fired up the blunt. He continuously exhaled the smoke in Ebony's direction eventually causing her eyes to become glassy. She laughed at everything he said and did to her. Soon, they were naked and christening every room in the house.

Ebony worked hard, in such a small amount of time, to make sure everything was in order for the small gathering of friends. The house was fully furnished and welcomed the ever-growing crowd that seemed to multiply by the minute.

All the men that were involved in the plan to be set forth in the next couple of days were present. None of the guests were strangers. There was a bond between everyone, and they all shared the same common goal—to find Rich. However, that night was the first time Dre had opened the doors to his new home. Once Ebony added the finishing touches, it looked like something from "*MTV Cribs*." The den had black marble floors and plasma TVs were on every wall, each showing a different section of the house.

The women watched the seventy-two-inch screen that showed them as they took turns going down their Soul Train line. They were all sexy and drunk as hell. The way they grinded and gyrated their hips was something

special. Each woman's eyes were on her man as she moved sensuously and erotically down the line toward her mate. The males were constantly distracted by the intended acts of their women.

The men watched the show, smoked top-of-the-line marijuana and drank the best cognac, but their main focus was on the TV screen that displayed the numerous stash spots belonging to Rich. They planned to hit each one in the upcoming days. They covered all the details to ensure that everything would go smoothly.

"Tony, is there anything on file at the precinct about any of these spots ever being raided before?" E asked.

"Not to my knowledge. You know that's a different jurisdiction, and any time that we enter that zone, it's with the OK from the commanding officer. I'll check on it though. Why? What's up?" Tony asked.

Dre spoke up. "Good, good," he said as he nodded his head. "We just don't need to be putting this down at the same time the police are conducting a surveillance or some shit, that's all."

"Well, I'll make a few calls to some contacts I got over that way and let you know." His willingness to be a part of such illegal activities impressed everyone.

"We straight on our end, bro law," E said. "We just need you on top of yours, making sure you inform us of any squads dispatched in that vicinity."

"That's no problem," Tony assured them. "I'll be close by, monitoring all transmissions out of that area."

"Well, it's a done deal then," said Eric.

Dee had been giving Tony the eye for a while. She was horny from the alcohol and was ready to get her freak on. She approached the men just as they were concluding their discussion.

"Um, excuse me," she said, clearing her throat. "Can I have my man back?" Drunkenly, she fell in Tony's lap.

"What's up, baby?" Tony asked as the rest of the guys laughed at her. Dre watched, admiring Tony's gentleness with his sister.

One by one, the women came to reclaim their men. Each pair retreated to a private room to start their own after-party, helping to relieve any stress before carrying out the plan.

NINE

Like clockwork, everyone was on time as they pulled into the back of the abandoned apartment building on the West Side. The station wagon that was to be used sat idling with its engine purring like a spinster's sewing machine. The body was rusted and dented but the tires were brand-new while the 451 big block would get them out of the area quickly in case something went wrong.

Silently, without any excess talking or noise, the six men secured the two personal vehicles they drove to the spot and climbed into the station wagon. They put on their bulletproof vests, checked their masks, loaded their guns and screwed on their silencers.

It was 2:30 a.m. when they passed Tony's unmarked

car on Lake Street. They flashed their lights quickly, signaling that their plan was in motion. Their destination was K-Town, a notorious gang-infested neighborhood on the West Side of Chicago. The neighborhood was easily recognized because all of the street names began with the letter K. That night, Kill Street would be added to the list, right behind Kildare if they appeared in alphabetical order.

As the station wagon turned onto Karlov, the house of interest came into view. Its position, one house from the corner, was custom built.

"Slow down right here and let me and Lucky out," E said from the back seat. "We'll give ya'll a few minutes to get around back."

They got out of the car and casually went the opposite direction to give the others time to get in place. Dre and A.D. would cover the back door. Future was the driver, while Lil Greg would pose as the dope-fiend, looking to cop some blow.

With guns out and ready, Dre and A.D. stood to the side as Lil Greg knocked on the door.

"Who is it?" a male voice demanded from the other side.

With his voice cracking and stuttering, Lil Greg responded, "It's Ronnie, man. I'm trying to do something. I got a grand."

The locks clicked and the door opened. A young dude appeared. "Nigga, don't be coming—"

Dre and A.D. busted past Lil Greg. Dre shot the doorman on sight as Lil Greg and A.D. proceeded through the house, looking for others. The element of surprise was on their side as they caught two men trying to get to their weapons.

"Police! Freeze!" A.D. hollered, stopping them in their tracks.

They threw them face down on the floor as Lil Greg went to open the front door for E and Lucky.

"What, wha—"

"Don't act like you don't know what it is. Where's the muthafuckin' dough, nigga?" Lucky shouted, kicking the closest victim in the head.

"Man, ain't no damn money in here!" one of them hollered.

"Oh yeah, it ain't, huh?" A.D. asked. He stepped up and shot him in the leg then turned to the other dude. "Let's try this again," he said, aiming the pistol at his head. "Where is the muthafuckin' money?"

"All right, man! The money is under the couch. There's a drop safe under the rug."

Lil Greg went to check and gave a nod. He pulled a cloth bag out of his jacket and put the money in it.

Dre squatted down next to the two men. "Check this out, I should blow your brains out," Dre said through clenched teeth as he pushed the pistol into the temple of one of the men. Hearing them gasp for air, he laughed. "What good would that do? Ya'll some lil

punk-ass bitches." He laughed at the sight of them quivering as he stood up.

"Duct tape them marks and let's ride. We been here long enough," E said.

Seven minutes after they entered, they were done. They stepped over the unconscious doorman and exited out of the back door where Future waited in the alley.

"Any problems?"

"None," Dre answered.

"Good," Future said as he turned the corner and headed for the next spot.

They planned to force Rich's hand by hitting most of his stash spots. They knew they couldn't break him but figured if they caused enough chaos and disruption, he'd surface.

Within hours, they hit four major houses with each producing more than the previous one. The dope they found was an added bonus. It was the beginning of dawn when they made it back to the South Side. Carrying eight cloth bags, they entered Dee's shop.

A short while later, Tony arrived. "How'd everything go?" he asked.

"So far so good," E responded, shaking Tony's hand. "Did you get any calls?"

"Nope. Nothing."

The men spent the next two and a half hours counting the money. The cocaine alone would bring in close

to three million dollars, coupled with the $4,684,559 in cash. Hopefully, it was enough to make Rich feel them.

Once the money and dope were divided, they gathered their weapons and put them in a bag to be destroyed.

"Handle that shit!" Rich yelled into his phone then slammed it shut. He was furious when he received the news about his stash houses being hit. One of the spots belonged to his uncle, and only one person knew about it—Dee Dee. He beat himself down for having ever taken her by there and pushed the Virgin Island cutie off of him. Reaching for the plate of cocaine, he shoveled a heap up his nose then pondered his next move.

He was in the middle of finalizing a multi-million dollar cocaine deal and resented being distracted with these latest developments. Having just left the states last week, he hadn't anticipated going back so soon. He had begun to enjoy the many amenities of St. Croix, including the cocaine and beautiful women, but he wanted to deal with this first hand.

Rich placed a call to Nine, who was in St. Thomas visiting a friend.

Nine picked up the phone on the first ring. "Yo yo," he answered. A live band could be heard in the background.

"What up, partna? Sounds like you having a good

time," Rich said, laughing a low, drug-induced chuckle. "Dig this, I hate to spoil the party, but we got some issues back on the home front that need to be handled, ASAP, nigga. How quick can you be here?"

Nine asked no questions. He concurred with anything Rich demanded. "Man, I think Seabourne Aviation got a seaplane leaving within an hour. You can meet me at the harbor around two."

"All right, it's a go," Rich said, terminating the call. His next call informed the hotel clerk that he was concluding his stay at the St. Croix by the Sea Hotel.

Atlanta's Hartsfield-Jackson International Airport was unusually crowded for October. Ebony was glad that it was the last leg of her assignment. She was still reveling in the excitement of Dre's proposal. She wanted to marry him right away, but she needed to be sure that he was ready and through with the streets. A voice invaded her thoughts.

"Excuse me, darling. How long before this plane takes off?"

Ebony turned to look at the intruder. It was something about the guy, and his friend, that she disliked on sight. Yet, she smiled. "Sir, as soon as the plane is serviced, we'll be on our way."

"I don't mean any disrespect," the man said, looking down at the ten-carat diamond engagement ring that damn near blinded him. "But you've got to be the most

beautiful woman I've seen all day. How about letting me spoil you for the weekend?"

"Sorry, I can't. I don't think my fiancé would approve of that," she said, looking for somewhere to escape. "If you would excuse me."

As she stood to leave, Rich offered his assistance. He placed his arm around her waist with his hand a lot lower than a stranger's was permitted.

"My, my, my," Rich crooned as he admired the plumpness of her ass.

Nine's eyes lit up as he too was mesmerized by Ebony's curves.

She removed Rich's arm from around her. "Look Mister, I'm trying to be professional and courteous in telling you to leave me the hell alone!" She was like a cat ready to strike. "And you shouldn't make a habit of putting your hands where they aren't wanted." She stormed off through a door marked "Employees Only," already realizing that it was going to be a long flight to Chicago.

TEN

"Dee Dee, I don't want you staying at that house by yourself anymore," Dre told her as he sifted the seeds out of the pound of weed on the table.

"I told you I got the locks changed."

"Changing locks ain't never stopped nobody from getting into a house."

"I've been trying to get her to move in with me," Tony spoke as he came up from the basement, carrying a case of Heineken.

"So, now I'm supposed to just up and sell my home?" Dee Dee asked. "I don't like this house," she said, looking around.

Ebony laughed at Dee Dee's honesty. She had to admit that Tony's three bedroom house was not a shack,

but it wasn't the most extravagant, either. However, everything about Dee Dee said high class. Ebony looked at the rocks on her fingers and the Prada outfit she was wearing and knew, for Tony, the road ahead was going to be a hard one to travel without the right ends.

"Well damn, is there anything else you don't like?"

"I'm sorry, baby. I didn't mean any harm," she apologized sincerely.

"I know you didn't, shorty. It's cool."

"Why don't both of you look for something better?" Dre asked.

"Yeah, something like you and E laying in? Right," Tony said, paying homage to the big boys.

Dre humbled himself and extended his helping hand. "I'm telling you, with that change you got the other night and the money from both houses, shit, that's a lot of miles from the hood. Dee still got the building to do something with. Sell it or rent it out." He decided not to mention the money he had put aside for her. The bottom line was he wanted her out of Rich's reach.

"I'll check around and see if I can find something I like," Dee said as she and Ebony disappeared into a back room.

"And don't be at that damn shop at night by yourself. Why are you still working there anyway?" Dre hollered behind her.

He puffed on the blunt of hydro and turned toward

Tony. "You know to holla at me if you need anything, right?"

"I think we got this, but I appreciate it though," Tony reassured, seeing a softer and more caring side of Dre. He knew that he'd gained his trust and wouldn't disappoint him.

◆ ◆ ◆

Rich's losses weren't his biggest issue. He was twisted by the fact that they pulled it off successfully. After dealing with the occupants of each house, he went to his North Side condo to put his plan in motion. He was humiliated, and he knew exactly who he wanted to feel the wrath of his retaliation.

As he revisited each intricate detail of his scheme, he became enthused by the idea of seeing her again. He reached for the phone and dialed. A woman spoke.

"Thank you for calling Simply Beautiful Hair Salon. How may I help you?"

"Is Dee Dee around?"

"Yes, please hold."

Rich hung up the phone, having gotten the answer he sought. He had one more call to make, to a number he didn't recognize.

◆ ◆ ◆

Monica looked like a wreck. She had done next to nothing the last couple of weeks but drown in the disappointment of how things played out with Dre. Her attempts to contact him were in vain. Several times, she

followed Dee Dee, hoping she would lead her to Dre since he seemed to have disappeared from the face of the earth. But her trail only led to Dee Dee's new man's house. Finally, she concluded the obvious, as if what he said at the funeral wasn't enough. He didn't want her. That was the most painful and humiliating part of it all. On top of rejecting her in front of his new woman after sleeping with her merely a few days before, the flat out dismissal of her as a person worthy of his attention was more than she could take. It was in this pain that the idea to make such a detrimental call was born. She held a grudge and believed in fighting fire with a blazing sword.

"Yo, who this?" Rich asked when a female voice answered the phone.

"Is this Rich?"

"No, this ain't Rich! Look lady, I don't got time to play games. Who is this and what the fuck you keep calling this number for?"

Monica's hands began to tremble, and she was tempted to hang up.

"My name is Monica," she said, hesitantly. "I was trying to speak to Rich. I have some information he could use."

He tried to place her name. It sounded familiar, but he couldn't pinpoint it.

"Info about what?"

"Look, I don't know who you are, but I'm trying to

talk to Rich. When you see him, tell him to give me a call." She was uncomfortable giving out information to the wrong person.

"Hey, hold up, Monica. Where did you meet Rich?"

"He's involved with the sister of my ex-boyfriend, and he tried to holla at me at the Fourth of July picnic."

The recollection of Monica came to him like a revelation. He remembered Dee Dee mentioning her once just before her brother came home.

"How about I have Rich meet you somewhere later on tonight?"

"Sure, as long as he makes it worth my while," she said, slowly forming a big payday in her mind.

"I'm sure that's no problem as long as the shit you got is on point, sweetheart."

Club Boye was crowded as Monica walked through the door. The music was loud and the flashing strobe lights made it difficult to focus on one person. Dressed casually in a low cut top, jeans and stilettos, she made her way to the bar. Heads turned as she walked past. She'd managed to pull herself together quickly, and regardless of how she felt on the inside, looked beautiful.

From the VIP section, Rich spotted her as she entered the club. He recognized her immediately from the picnic. Although she wasn't as fine as Dee Dee, she looked good. He visualized fucking her as he made his

way to the bar.

"What's up, beautiful," he said by way of introduction. He slid next to her. "To what do I owe such a pleasant encounter?"

Surprised, Monica jumped at his voice so close in her ear. However, she played it off well by giving him a sexy smile. She didn't realize that he was such a handsome man before that moment. With his caramel-colored skin, alluring eyes and perfect white teeth inside of a million-dollar smile, one would never know that he was a beast. Dressed in the finest of linen with a three-quarter-length lambskin leather jacket, Rich was indeed attractive. His bling—ten-carat round diamond earrings (five in each ear), a diamond encrusted "R" wearing a crown hanging from a platinum chain, the Jacob and Co. watch and two invisible set diamond pinky rings—added to his aura. Instantly, she decided to make the best of this meeting.

"Like I said to you on the phone, I believe we can help each other," she responded.

"Go on," he said as he gave her his undivided attention.

"As you know, until recently, I was involved with Dre."

"What happened? Why the change of heart?" he questioned.

"I'm really not comfortable talking about this in here. Is there somewhere we can go that's a little more

private?" she asked, playing right into his hand.

"I have a place not too far from here. How does that sound?" He traced a finger down her thigh.

"That sounds wonderful," she replied with a devilish smile.

♦ ♦ ♦

Back at his condo, Monica got comfortable as she and Rich exchanged pleasantries.

"Would you like something to drink?"

"Yes, thank you," she responded.

While at the bar, Rich watched Monica swaying to the music. As he mixed her drink, he dropped in an ecstasy pill and stirred to dissolve it. He wanted to be sure he extracted all viable information from her and then some.

He sat next to her as they discussed the events of the last few weeks. She was reluctant at first, and he understood this was her strategy. Along with the satisfaction of paying Dre back, she wanted money.

"How do I know this isn't a game you're playing?"

"Be serious. Would I…risk being here with you…you if I wasn't serreeus?" Monica slurred her words as the combination of alcohol and X took effect.

"OK, let's get right to the point. How much?"

Without a second thought, she blurted out, "Fifty thousand."

Rich smiled, not fazed by the amount but by her greed.

"That's not a problem…with a little added incentive," he said as he slowly unbuttoned her shirt, looking into her hazed eyes. "Let's discuss this somewhere more comfortable."

He led her into the all green, pleasure-seeking ambience of his bedroom and laid her across the bed with a plethora of pillows, 1000-thread-count Egyptian cotton sheets and a down comforter folded back toward the foot. With the lights dimmed, music softly playing and the hidden cameras activated, he undressed her while nibbling and softly sucking on her breasts.

Monica was ready to seal the deal as she reached for his dick. "Come here and give me some of that big dick," she demanded, stroking it roughly in her palm.

"Not so fast, baby. We got the whole night ahead of us. Let's take our time," he said as he reached into the leather case that sat on the green marble nightstand. He retrieved a vibrator the color of the Incredible Hulk.

With it still off, he rubbed it up and down her pussy as she steadily stroked his penis.

He pushed the head of the toy inside of her. He was pleasantly surprised at the ease with which it entered. She was wet, willing and ready. Feeling the vibrator inside of her, she released a soft, purring sound while massaging her nipples with her forefinger and thumb. Turning it on, he inched it deep inside of her hole.

"Ooh, that feels good," she said, squirming, trying to push it deeper. Her milky colored juices coated the green rubber dick as she spread her legs, allowing him greater access to her pussy.

He pulled the vibrator out of her and ran it across her lips. "Ummm...delicious," she said as she kissed the head before taking it all into her mouth. Rich was fully erect as he pleasured Monica. He removed the vibrator from her mouth then positioned himself so she could suck his dick. Placing his hands on both sides of her head and running his fingers through her long, silky hair, he slid his thick dick into her mouth then guided her head up and down its shaft. Like a possessed demon, she accepted all of him.

Next, Monica was on her back. He took her legs in his arms and pulled her to the edge of the mattress, leaving her shoulders as the only part of her body still on the bed. He opened her legs wider, causing the pussy lips to spread. Grabbing his dick, he moved the head back and forth, stimulating her clitoris. As he entered, Monica went into a frenzy then arched her back, accepting him.

"Oh shit! Oh! Oh! Oh!" she yelled in unison with squeaking mattress as he pounded her. Her titties, perfect in stature, bounced to the rhythm. "Ohh, it feels so good! Fuck me harder! I'm about to cum!" she screamed.

Rich pulled out and ejaculated on her pussy, letting his semen run down the crack of her ass. He turned her over and reached for the K-Y to lubricate her asshole.

"No, don't do that," she said after realizing his intention. Her words went unheard as he spread her cheeks with his thumbs. Surprisingly, he entered her ass without much pain or resistance. Before long, Monica was pushing backward, accepting him and wanting more. "I can't believe…I'm about to cum again," she said as she rose up on her hands. Pushing her back down on the bed, Rich grabbed her ass and hiked it up a little more as he exploded.

Monica spent the night with Rich. She earned every dime of the fifty thousand, giving all of herself and the information. The next morning she left with an envelope filled with money and a sore body but no regrets. She needed the cash since she gave Dre the seventy-five hundred dollars, her life savings. She had anticipated winning him back with it, but he had only rejected her.

ELEVEN

Dee Dee had been out and about all day while Tony was working late. Daylight saving time was long gone, so darkness fell quick in the month of November. Having found a couple of houses that suited her taste, Dee wanted to look at them before heading home. But she had to hurry because later on that night she and Tony planned on having dinner with Dre and Ebony. She was so occupied that she never even noticed the car following her. As the street and headlights came on, she couldn't distinguish one vehicle from the other even if she wanted to.

Whether it was her sixth sense or some strange premonition, Dee was no longer comfortable out alone after nightfall by herself. She glanced in her rearview

mirror. The bright lights of a car behind her shone in her eyes. Staying with the flow of the Dan Ryan traffic, she exited on 79th and headed east toward Tony's South Shore neighborhood.

Dee Dee saw the Walgreens up ahead and remembered the film she'd dropped off earlier. She was reminded of the good time they had at her brother's house so on the spur of the moment, she decided to pick up the pictures. Getting out of the car and walking into the drugstore, she called to ask Tony if he needed anything.

There were only a few customers, so she was in and out in a flash. From the moment she left the store, it seemed as though everything slowed down, and she had entered into a bad dream. She shifted the bag with the pictures and two bottles of Chardonnay into her other hand as she fumbled with her keys. The hair on the nape of her neck stood on ends as her senses sent her one last warning. Had she taken off running, she would've escaped her kidnapper. Instead, she chanced a peek over her shoulder and that's when the strange man spoke.

"Don't scream if you want to live," he said as he wrapped a powerful arm around her, pulling her close to him. With his other hand he pushed the gun into her side. "Everything will be all right, lady. Don't be stupid." All of a sudden, she couldn't see anymore.

A Yukon pulled up next to them and she was thrown

into the back, blindfolded.

It was well into the evening when Ebony pulled into their driveway in her brand new silver Range Rover. Having let the lease expire on her apartment, this was officially home. They had set a wedding date for Valentine's Day.

Dre, in his own car, had been following her but needed to make a quick stop. As she sat in the car waiting for him, she decided to address the envelopes and money orders to his homies on lock down. She admired that he never forgot about them.

The roar of the Viper's engine and the screeching of its tires as Dre flew into the driveway frightened Ebony. He was on the phone. Anger and alarm were clearly visible on his face and in his voice.

She dropped what she was doing and ran to the car where he sat, barking into the phone. "DeAndre, what's wrong? What happened?" she asked on the verge of tears. She knew it was pretty bad.

"I just spoke with her earlier and she said that you all would be by here later. It's not like her to just up and disappear, and not answer her phone," Dre said. "When was the last time you saw her, Tony?"

"I spoke with her a couple of hours ago and everything was all right. She was on 79th Street and said that she was going to make a quick stop at Walgreens and then go straight home. I haven't heard from her since. I

got a couple of squad cars checking that Walgreens and a few more drug stores in that area. If we get something, I'll get right at you."

"Bet! In the meantime, I'm going back out to see what I can come up with. Call me as soon as you hear something," Dre said, closing the phone.

"DeAndre, what's wrong? What happened to Dee Dee?" Ebony demanded, already knowing from the gist of their conversation.

Dre stepped out of the car and pulled Ebony into his arms. "I'm not sure, baby. No one seems to know where Dee Dee is and she's not answering her phone. Maybe it's nothing. She probably left her phone somewhere or turned it off by mistake," Dre said, trying to reassure himself as he held Ebony tight in his arms.

"How long will you be gone, Dre?" she asked, snuggling her head into his chest. "I'm scared to stay in this big house by myself."

"Baby, I won't be gone too long. I'm sure it's nothing, like I said. I just need to be positive, that's all," he responded. He kissed her. "Do you mind if I take your truck?"

"You can drive anything you want as long as you make it back safely," she said, kissing him passionately.

She watched him leave. "Call me to let me know what's going on!" she yelled. *God, please don't let this be the last time I see him*, she said to herself then recited a silent prayer for Dee Dee that God would watch over her, if,

in fact, something was wrong.

Monica was in bed, asleep all day, since she made it home from her night with Rich. Her body was hurting from the sexual beating he put on her. After a certain point, everything about that night was a blur and even now, she still suffered from lightheadedness. But it was nothing fifty thousand dollars couldn't cure.

Finally, she got out of bed, showered, dressed and decided to treat herself to something special. Her first stop was the Honda dealership where she traded in her car for a brand new Honda Accord LX. From there, she bought some furniture, and as dusk sneaked up on her, she decided to get her hair done.

As it was so late in the day, everyone was booked for the rest of the evening, even her regular beautician who didn't care how much of a tip Monica offered because she was working on her last client. On the spur of the moment, she drove toward Simply Beautiful, the place where Dee Dee worked, to see if they could take her as a walk-in.

From the parking lot she knew something was wrong and her heart began to flutter. Her hands trembled when she saw Dre for the first time in weeks, emerging from the shop. His pace was intense and hurried. He walked toward some guys huddled around a new truck. She recognized Eric. Looking closer at the other guy, she tried to place him. *Oh, that's the guy who was*

at the picnic with Dee Dee. I wonder why he's carrying a gun, she thought as she noticed it was secured in a holster around his waist. She also made a mental note of the police badge hanging from a chain around his neck. She sat and observed for a minute, making sure she wasn't driving into the middle of a major drug bust. After a while, she realized they were friends.

Not wanting to appear nervous or suspicious, she went along with her initial plans. She parked and got out of her car. The noise from her driver side door shutting caused them to look her way.

Monica's presence was as out of place as a preacher in a strip joint. No one could find reason for her being there. As she approached, all eyes were on her.

"Why is everyone looking like they saw a ghost?" she asked as she stood in front of them.

"Have you seen Dee?"

"Well, hello to you too, Dre. No, I haven't seen or spoken to Dee Dee in over a month," she responded, never making eye contact with either of them. "Has anyone checked her house?"

"Why would we have to check her house?" Dre questioned with an arched eyebrow.

"Maybe, she went back to check—" She caught her mistake too late. She wouldn't have known that Dee Dee wasn't staying there if she hadn't spoken to her in a month.

They all caught her slip, but Tony beat them to the

punch. "Monica, how did you know Dee Dee don't stay at her house anymore?"

She tried to straighten up her blunder. "I don't! I just figured that if ya'll been together since I first saw ya'll at the picnic, things must be to that point." She was nervous and ready to leave. "I didn't know you were the police," she stated, trying to shift the focus.

"That's of no concern to you," Dre said. "But what is, is you popping up out of the blue. Why are you here?" He saw something in her eyes that he couldn't put his finger on.

"Yeah, I want to hear this, too," E chimed in.

"My beautician was booked, and since I was in the area, I decided to see if someone over here could fit me in. Ya'll acting like I'm responsible for her disappearing."

"I never said she disappeared." Dre was trying his best to get Monica to confess that she knew something was going on.

Oh shit, Monica thought to herself.

"You know what, Mo, for your sake, nothing better be wrong with my sister. 'Cause if I find out something is, and you knew about it, I'ma bury yo' ass six feet deep." Dre gave warning. His voice was soft and far away while his mind was trying to put the pieces together. He looked at the car, noticing it was new. "Oh, and by the way, that's a nice car you got," he said. "You got a job or some stupid nigga throwing bricks for your

ass?"

She peered at him through squinted eyes and diverted her gaze over his shoulder at the Range Rover. "Thanks, but yours is better. Wanna trade?" she interjected, ignoring his comment.

Everybody glared at her.

"Well, I have to be going. If I hear anything, I'll let you know, DeAndre. Call me if you need me," she said, using the opportunity to exit.

After the strange encounter with Monica, they went to search Dee Dee's car. They found it in the Walgreens parking lot. The clerk in the store remembered her, but didn't recall anything out of the ordinary.

The men rode in silence throughout the night, searching for Dee Dee. The thought of her being dead hung at the back of each of their minds.

"We should file a missing persons report," Tony suggested but got no response. "It can't hurt!"

"That won't do no good. We know exactly what happened to Dee, and we all know that it has something to do with that bitch-ass nigga Rich!" Dre was consumed with anger. "I told her ass not to be out by herself. Damn it!" He slammed his palm against the steering wheel.

"Wasn't that bitch acting crazy as hell?" E asked, reflecting on their encounter with Monica.

"Something ain't right with her. Usually she would

be pressing all up on you, homie."

"Yeah, I feel you. It was like we caught her off-guard or something. I just can't figure it out," Dre said.

Tony sat in the back in deep thought. "Does anybody know where that nigga's spot is on the North Side? I say we pay his ass a visit."

"We will…in due time," Eric responded. "In due time."

TWELVE

Dee Dee lay across the bed, blindfolded and tied up. The smell of fresh linens surprised her, but the presence of someone hovering over was as heavy as shopping bags after a day at the mall with Rich. A light and gentle hand caressed the side of her face. "Don't touch me," she spat.

The same hand that was just so gentle, sent a burst of stars through her head. "Shut up, bitch!"

A light whimper escaped her lips as the front of her blouse was snatched open. "Please—"

Before she could utter another word, she took another blow to her dome. It silenced her. She wasn't wearing a bra and the air quickly hardened her nipples.

"I want you to listen and listen well," the muffled

voice instructed her. "You do nothing and say nothing unless I say so."

Somewhere within the distorted voice was some familiarity. She wanted to say his name, but remembered his warning, so she remained quiet.

Moments later, she was spread eagle on her back, completely naked and blindfolded with her hands tied above her head. Her legs were free and she crossed them, trying to cover herself as well as protect what belonged to Tony.

She sensed him close to her again and the cold steel of the pistol as he moved it over her body confirming his proximity.

"Open your legs," he said. The threat of the weapon was enough persuasion.

She felt the hot breath then the wet and slippery tongue as it slithered up the inside of her thighs. The technique was so familiar.

"First things first," he whispered as his tongue entered her.

She fought the excitement and pleasant sensations as best she could but was forced into an unwanted orgasm. It was moments before her breathing returned to normal.

"Don't ever underestimate what I say, Dee Dee!" he spoke in his own voice.

"Rich, why are you doing this?" she chanced. "What have I ever done to you?"

"Bitch, you betrayed me, used me and disrespected me! I can go on and on! Then, your brother challenged my character and that of my men. Don't act like you don't know what happened." He removed the blindfold. "And you start fucking with a muthafuckin' cop! What the fuck were you thinking 'bout?"

As her eyes adjusted to the light, she said, "Rich, my brother never did anything to you and neither have I. How can he not try to protect me?"

He cocked the gun and pointed it at her head.

"Do you think I'm stupid? Huh? You were the only person that knew about that one spot, Dee Dee!" Spit flew out of his mouth as his anger was building. With his free hand, he sent a punishing blow to her jaw, knocking her out. "Bitch, you owe me!"

Dre sat in his den, staring past the flat screen on the wall. Neither the posh surroundings nor the expensive trimmings could fill the empty place in his heart caused by the mere thought of his sister being dead. All day, he fought with the idea of Tony involving the police. Each time he shot it down. He believed that real niggas kept street shit where it belonged. He would relinquish all he owned to know that Dee Dee was alive and in the safety of his confines. Yet, he didn't know where to begin the search for his sister. He reached for the photo of Dee Dee and Rich, wanting to look into his eyes and connect with him in some way. Then he looked at Dee

Dee, and underneath her smile, he saw a hint of fear.

Ebony walked into the room and handed Dre a beer as she sat next to him. "What are you…"

Ring…Ring…

"Hello?" Ebony said as she cradled the phone between her ear and neck while she stroked Dre's fingers.

"Hey. How ya'll holding up over there?" Eric asked.

"As well as expected. Have you heard anything yet?"

"Nope, nothing."

"Damn!" she said quietly under her breath. "Hold on. Here's Dre." She handed him the phone.

"What's up, nigga," Dre said, sounding sullen.

"Come on man, we gonna handle this. We both know, quiet as it's kept, the nigga ain't gonna kill her. He's gonna use her to get to you," E said, trying to lift his spirits with a little reasoning.

"E-Mo, this the same nigga that was punching her in the eye and kicking her ass for no reason! I ain't buying that, homie."

"Have faith, nigga! Oh, and I got the passkey to that condo on the North Side. We're gonna check it tonight, bet?"

"Bet," Dre said, hanging up the phone. He took another good look at the picture then turned to Ebony. Her eyes and mouth were wide open as she stared at the photo.

"What you looking like that for?"

She pointed her finger. "Is that Rich?" she inquired. "Tell me it ain't," she begged, while placing her head on his chest.

"That's the nigga. Why?"

"A while ago, he flew from Atlanta with me."

"Where was he coming from?"

"I think the Caribbean Islands, but I know he is downright disgusting and he got a serious hand problem!"

Dre didn't show an inkling of anger because his mind was in overdrive like his Viper on the highway during the wee hours of morning. "If you ever see him again, let me know." He didn't think she would, knowing he wanted to kill Rich. He knew she wasn't cut out for the life but was truly wifey material.

They kissed and then sat in silence, each in their own thoughts. She looked at him, wanting to say something but didn't. He felt her vibe. "What's up, Ebony? Talk to me."

She continued to look at him quietly. "You know, every time I see you I smile because I love you so much, and I know you are a good person, but your life is so uncertain, sweetie. I find myself holding my breath from day to day not knowing if it will be the last day I see you. Now, I know that we have to try and find Dee Dee, and I'm with you on that, but I'm through after this."

"Through?" Dre questioned.

"Yeah. I want us to lead a simple and quiet life."

Dre discharged a sigh of relief. He thought she was actually trying to call off their engagement.

"With a bunch of babies?" he asked, relieved, rubbing her ass.

"Yeah, and a bunch of years with my man."

"Your man? How about *husband*," he joked.

"You're absolutely right…once this is over. We both know the ending ain't guaranteed to be in our favor, and I know that you will risk your life for your sister. But where does that leave me if something happens to you?"

At that moment, he felt something he had never sensed before. He knew she was the woman he wanted, without a shadow of a doubt, and believed it was his duty, his obligation, to always love and care for her.

"I wish I could say that you're wrong, but I can't. The only thing I can promise is that it's a wrap after this. We'll get married, take a long vacation for the honeymoon and try to make a couple of babies or have fun trying." He stared back into her eyes, smiling.

Dre had been thinking the same thing that Ebony verbalized. Life was meant to be so much easier. It wasn't meant for niggas to be out here taking deadly or penitentiary chances. In such a short time, he had acquired enough money to do whatever he wanted to do with his life. He was set up to live decent and comfortable. It was niggas on the streets that never did a day

in jail but continued to live hand to mouth. He was fortunate and lucky enough to rise above the poverty that so many Black people succumbed to on a daily basis. After processing his thoughts, he wondered why, day after day, his life was still a gamble.

Traffic, going north, was steady. The leaves on the trees were long gone and the cold of winter was in the air. The Range Rover blended in well with the expensive cars belonging to people existing within the upper echelons of society—Chicago's elite. Never knowing life at a lesser degree, they literally owned the North Side.

Dre and Eric spoke less as they tried to anticipate any complications with the job ahead. Although they knew it was a long shot, they needed to be for sure. That's why they chose such a busy time of day, hoping they wouldn't look too suspicious. After all, there were a few Blacks that lived there, Rich being one.

E swiped the pass through the scanner and the indicator light turned green. The gate opened, allowing them access to the exclusive community. A few residents were jogging, but none paid attention to them. They were in the condo in record time. With guns drawn, they searched for occupants. It was obvious someone had been there recently because two glasses, with melted ice water, sat on the table.

"Nobody," E informed Dre, coming back into the room. "Let's do a quick sweep to see what we can find."

"Yeah, we might run across something," Dre said as he began opening doors.

At the same time, Dre searched the front while E looked through a back bedroom and came up with a handful of tapes. There was a camera and monitor still set up, so he selected a tape and put it in.

The picture came up kind of distorted at first, but eventually it cleared and a female appeared on the screen. She was naked on a bed with money surrounding her. "Hey Dre, check this out!" E hollered toward the front of the condo.

Dre came into the room and froze. "What the fuck is that?" he asked. He was shocked by the image on the monitor.

Looks like a homemade flick to me," Eric said, looking through the other tapes. "This is an old tape. Look at the date at the bottom," he continued, trying not to watch what Dee Dee was doing.

"Turn that shit off, man! I don't wanna see my sister naked! You look like you enjoying the bullshit! We both know she's...just like any other female," Dre said. "Ain't nobody here. Let's go!"

"Hold up."

"Hold up my ass! Let's go! Ain't nobody here."

E found another tape. "Will you wait a minute? This one is more recent." He put the tape in and another woman appeared. She, too, was across the bed.

Dre looked like he had seen a ghost, as he stood with

his mouth open. He knew that ass like he knew his own. In a trance, he watched as Rich undressed Monica. He knew she was trifling but never thought she could be so malicious and spiteful.

There was total silence in the room as they watched the freak show worthy of a best actress award from the Academy.

Unbelieving, E shook his head. "Ain't that a bitch!"

Dre said nothing. He just watched and stared back into Monica's eyes as she looked directly into the camera. She looked wasted and fucked up. "Can you believe this shit? The audacity of this bitch! I knew when her ass showed up that night at the shop that something just wasn't right. Man, I swear to God I'm gon' kill that bitch if she's got anything to do with this shit."

"Let's go get to the bottom of this," Eric said as he gathered all the tapes.

THIRTEEN

Monica had been trying to get in contact with Rich all day. When the realization of her actions set in, she felt a tinge of sorrow and guilt. The thought of something terrible happening to Dee Dee left her regretting the moves she had made. She kept having flashbacks of Dee Dee running to her rescue during the altercation with Dre at his party.

She was sitting by the phone, waiting for Rich to call her back.

Knock...knock...knock!

She jumped as someone banged on the door repeatedly. Creeping to the door with her heart thumping loudly, she peeped through the curtains.

Dre banged again, and each knock sounded as

though the door would fly off its hinges.

"Monica, you got five seconds to open this mutha-fuckin' door before I kick it down!"

She slowly turned the locks, all the time wondering if he knew she had fucked Rich.

"Stop bangin' on my door like that, DeAndre," she said in an authoritative tone. Dre wasn't backing down because he had the evidence in his jacket. As the last lock was opened, he burst through the door, sending her reeling backwards to fall on the couch. He walked over to her, grabbed her by the jaw, lifted her from the couch then pushed her against the wall. His hand slid down around her neck.

With the corner of his mouth turned up in disgust, Dre looked at her. "How long have you been fuckin' that nigga?"

Tears ran down her face. She knew he'd found out, somehow, and was too scared to lie. "Just once, DeAndre. I swear," she whispered as she began to cry.

Not a word was uttered as he struggled to deal with the deceit he felt. His mouth was dry and palms were sweaty. It was as though he couldn't control his hands as they tightened around her neck.

The vessels in Monica's eyes were starting to burst as she tried to break his grip. "Arrgh! Arrgh! Arrgh!" she murmured. Spittle ran down the sides of her mouth.

He released her, and she fell to the floor, coughing.

Slowly, her resentment became hatred. She stood

and charged at him. "It's all your fault, DeAndre!" She pounded his chest until she got tired. "Why did you fuck me if you knew you didn't want to be with me? I love you, DeAndre. I've never stopped loving you. You were the best man to ever come into my life. I know I was wrong. But, I hoped you could forgive me. You didn't have to dog me in front of some girl you don't even know that well, DeAndre. I thought we were better than that."

When she was through with her mini-tantrum, he slapped her to the ground. "Do you know where Dee Dee is?" He pulled the stun gun from the small of his back. "Answer me, bitch! I need to know that you didn't have nothing to do with Dee Dee's disappearance." The sound of electricity from the instrument was terrifying as he squatted down beside her. "Where is Dee Dee?" he asked again as the two prongs touched her bare leg, sending twenty thousand volts of electricity through her body.

"Aahhhhhhh!" Monica screamed at the top of her lungs. "I don't know what you're talking about, Dre," she said, squealing from the pain. He touched her again, this time leaving it for a few lingering, excruciating seconds until she passed out. He carried her to the bed and settled into the recliner, anticipating a long night. He watched the tape of her again, in its entirety.

♦ ♦ ♦

Dee Dee heard the voices, but she kept her eyes

closed. She recognized the second voice as Nine's. She did all she could not to move and was still naked with her legs slightly open. She knew she was at their mercy so appearing to be embarrassed wouldn't stop them from looking, touching or doing whatever else they wanted to her. So she ignored the breeze between her legs and listened.

"You couldn't get them to hold off for a minute?" Rich asked Nine.

"You know how them cats think their business is the most important shit in the world," Nine responded. "I tried to get something scheduled for a couple weeks from now, but they wouldn't go for it."

Rich sat thinking. "Damn, I wanted to handle this bitch and her brother first. What type of figures did ya'll come up with?"

With lust in his eyes, Nine wasn't listening. He was preoccupied with Dee Dee's pussy. "Huh? What you say, cuz?"

"I asked how much. But I see you got other things on your mind." He shook his head as he glanced at her, too.

"You might as well try her out before we off her punk ass," Rich said, laughing wickedly.

Nine moved closer to Dee Dee. He reached out, rubbing her breasts. "They're asking five and a half and that's with the drop in Miami. It seems someone got over on them recently cause they want the cash a day in

advance." His dick was hardening as he fondled her titties.

"Maybe I can shoot down there in a day or two. Can you handle things here while I'm gone?"

"I can hold down the fort till you get back. But I must say, I don't know how long I can curb this desire to put my dick in her mouth."

"I don't think I'd try that," Rich laughed. "You'll fuck around and draw back a nub. Although, I must say, the bitch's head game is flawless, but don't underestimate her."

"So, you want me to give the go ahead?"

"Yeah, and reserve one round trip to St. Croix for me."

"You got that, playa!" Nine said as he left.

"Make sure they understand it's gonna be a few days from now," Rich hollered behind Nine.

He walked over to where Dee Dee was lying and watched her while letting his thoughts run rampant. He felt a pang of sorrow because, in his own psychotic way, he loved her.

"You might as well open your eyes, you ain't asleep," he said as he untied her. "I want you to make a phone call to your punk-ass brother and tell him that he owes me ten million, and he ain't got a whole lot of time to get it to me, either."

"Rich, Dre don't have that type of money," she pleaded, although she did think he might actually have

it. If not, Eric did.

"He better find it then! Besides, don't think I haven't heard how he got the South Side on lock. That good boy is laying them dope fiends out. And if all else fails, he got my money. Remember?" He sat next to her admiring her body.

"Can I put some clothes on, please? It's cold in here." The look on his face left her unsure of her destiny, but she saw the odds of escaping increase when she noticed the gun on top of the dresser. Just that quick, her instincts turned to fight or flight. She knew she couldn't fight Rich and win, but she was willing to try the next best thing. She reached out and rubbed his thigh, close to his crotch. "How can you love me and do me like this, Rich?" she spoke.

"Man, I don't wanna hear that bullshit." He waved her comment off.

"I'm for real. I thought me and you had something. I would have never thought in a million years that things would come to this."

"What did you expect? When your brother came home, you changed—started acting like you didn't need a nigga and disrespecting me."

"Rich…I was always thankful for what you did for me, but I didn't want to be possessed and controlled. I only wanted to be loved." As Dee Dee looked at him intently, Rich turned away. "And sometimes I felt like your jealousy overshadowed what you felt for me. But I

understand now you really do love me. You do still love me, Rich, don't you?" She reached out for him, pulling him toward her. He offered no resistance.

"You know I love you."

"Show me how much you love me then," she whispered.

Soon, Rich was naked, on top of Dee Dee. As he entered her, the familiarity of her pussy had his nose wide open once again. She gave him her all as she put her legs on his shoulders. She met his every thrust because her survival depended on it. Perhaps she would get an opportunity to get to the gun. "Ummm," she moaned as she began to sense a familiar sensation in between her legs. "Let me get on top, Rich," she whispered. "I've been missing this dick."

Rich lay on his back, waiting for her to mount him. She took her time, as if she was getting ready for the second round, then broke for the gun.

Grabbing it she pointed the pistol at him. "If you come anywhere near me I swear to God I will kill you!" Her hands were shaking terribly. "All I want to do is get the fuck out of here."

Rich did not hesitate in his pursuit to reach Dee Dee. "What the fuck I just say! Don't come any closer!" Dee Dee warned. He continued toward her, as she kept backing up, until she was against the wall.

"Stop, damnit!" When the distance narrowed she closed her eyes and pulled the trigger. Nothing hap-

pened.

Rich laughed at her and shook his head.

After several attempts to fire, she realized the clip wasn't in the gun. "GODDAMNIT!" she cried and slumped to the floor.

"Did you actually think I would be stupid enough to leave a loaded gun sitting out in plain view?" He snatched the nickel-plated nine-millimeter out of her hand. "Get yo' dumb ass up and finish what you started!" He yanked her up off of the floor and threw her on the bed face down. Trying to squirm to get away, he grabbed her legs. They damn near broke as he spread them apart.

"Rich, please don't—" she yelled.

"Please don't," he mimicked in a high-pitched tone.

"Ahhhhh!!!" Dee Dee yelled as she felt a sharp pain.

Rich pounded his dick into her ass without any reserve, ignoring her cries. It was uncomfortable for him at first because he used no lubrication, but the mere thought of what he was doing masked the initial discomfort. He found a good rhythm then opened her cheeks to get a look at his dick going in and out of her asshole. Just as he was about to cum he pushed her head into the pillows to silence her screams. Dee Dee was unable to move. After he came, he withdrew his dick and saw cum mixed with blood. "You stupid bitch!" he growled then brought the butt of the gun down across her head. He left her unconscious in a puddle of blood.

♦ ♦ ♦

Close to a week had passed, and they were no closer to finding Dee Dee. Her disappearance was taking a toll on Dre. He could only hope she was alive. There was no balance, no peace and no certainties. His sister was the only family he had left so he would do anything—pay any price—to get her back. He amazed himself, not killing Monica. Although, it took every ounce of strength he had to refrain. She begged and pleaded with him, insisting that she was drugged. He knew she was lying but above and beyond that, he needed her alive to help locate Rich.

Sleep had avoided Dre for a few days. He would lie in bed with his eyes wide open, trying to formulate a course of action. On one particular day, he was partaking of his morning ritual—listening to a talk show on satellite radio while smoking a blunt. Ebony was due to fly out in a couple of hours so that added to his dismal mood. He couldn't convince her to quit.

Ring...Ring...

Dre rushed to the phone so it wouldn't wake Ebony up. *Who is calling at this time?* he thought to himself. *When phones ring this early, it only means one of two things.*

"Hello?" His heart pounded as he answered.

"Dre, please help me! He's gonna kill me!" the voice on the other end whimpered.

"Dee Dee, where are you?" Her fragile and broken voice crushed him. "Are you all right? Did he hurt you?" He had a thousand questions, none of which got answered because the phone was snatched away from her.

"That's enough, Bitch!" Rich put the phone to his ear. "Yo Dre?" he asked.

"Check this out, Rich, if you—"

"No, you check this out, punk-ass nigga! The only thing you should be doing is listening to my directions on where to drop ten million, if you want this bitch back! Do you understand, nigga?"

"Yeah, aight, I hear you," Dre replied, biting his tongue.

"Good! You don't sound so muthafuckin' tough now," Rich added for insult.

Dre didn't trust speaking and didn't want to further agitate him, so he waited on the directions.

"I want ten million cash, unmarked, all hundred-dollar bills."

"Man, I ain't sitting on that kind of money! You know that!" Veins started showing on Dre's forehead.

"Nigga, you got just about that much from me, so save that bullshit. You either have it by midnight tomorrow, or kiss baby girl goodbye! Now, do I need to continue or what?" he asked, waiting for a response.

Dre's mind was working, calculating how much money he had, how much he needed and where to get it. His hands were tied. He knew Rich had one up on him.

"Where do you want the money? And I need to see Dee before I drop."

"Didn't I tell you to shut the fuck up? I'm the one callin' the shots around here nigga, not you! I want the money dropped on Lake Street and Homan Avenue at the old Gayhawks Motorcycle Club. You can't miss it. There's an entrance door around back. Drop the money right inside the door and leave. Do not attempt to enter the building."

"Yo, but what about my sister? How do I even know she'll still be alive?"

"There's a McDonald's around the corner. Once I give the OK, my men will drop her there. Remember, any funny shit, and she dies. Oh, and leave Officer Friendly at home. You really are a stupid-ass nigga." The line disconnected.

Dre didn't know if Lucky, A.D. or Future could better the odds of getting Dee Dee back, but their presence was always welcomed. He called and brought them abreast of the latest happenings. They felt like they needed to be there for Dre as he was for them since one hand washes the other. They planned to be in town early the next morning, just in case.

FOURTEEN

No one knew of the reprimands Tony had received at work. He had been written up several times for conduct unbecoming of an officer, failure to follow orders and jurisdiction deviation.

Unbeknownst to any of the others, Tony and a few of his co-workers had been riding through the West Side, ruffling feathers while trying to get a lead on Rich. An altercation with one of the local hustlers resulted in multiple injuries that sent him to the intensive care unit at Cook County Hospital. After an investigation was conducted, Tony was identified as the officer in question, and a police brutality suit was filed against him. But it didn't matter. Saving Dee Dee was all he could think about. He had a substantial amount of

money saved, not including his take from the robberies. He wanted his woman back at any and all costs.

Dre called to let Tony know that he had spoken to Dee and informed him of the ten-million-dollar ransom. The mention of such a large amount of money diminished his hopes, at first. He never knew how much money went through Dre's hand but when Dre informed him that he and E were ready to make the drop tomorrow night, his spirits began to soar. They all would meet, a couple hours before midnight the following day, to discuss the best way to recover Dee Dee.

After concluding the conversation with Dre, Tony reclined in his chair, sinking into deep thought. His partner watched him from the door.

"Tony, I'm starting to worry about you. You haven't been yourself for the last week or so. You want to talk about it?" a fellow officer asked.

"Is it that obvious?" he said, rubbing his head.

"Yeah, it's obvious."

"Man, I'm just dealing with some personal issues and it's stressing me the hell out," Tony replied, slapping the desk. "But don't worry about me. I'll be cool."

"Hey, I forgot to tell you. I overheard Lieutenant Moody talking to the captain about an officer who is allegedly affiliated with some drug dealer. He was observed at a picnic, or somewhere with him, awhile back."

Tony's demeanor didn't give away his interest in his

friend's words. Tactfully, he needed to know more. "Is that so? Do they have anything incriminating on him?"

"That's just it. Supposedly, there was this lady who was supplying the information, but she's nowhere to be found. So, without her, ain't no case. Anyway, we don't have nothing to worry about, right?" he asked suspiciously.

"Nothing at all. And thanks for checking on me."

"No problem," his partner said as he left the office. "Call me if you need me for anything." With one last look, directly into Tony's eyes, he closed the door behind him.

Tony held his head in his hands, trying to stop the constant pounding. It didn't take much to figure out that Monica was the informant. He realized he might have to pay her a visit.

With Ebony gone for eight days, Dre was home alone on the day of the transaction. He was in bed, awake for so long that he decided to get up and start breakfast for the crew due in from Milwaukee. E called from the expressway and was expected any minute.

Coming up with ten million cash was no small feat. The amount, with the help of E, was no drawback. However, the requested denomination proved to be problematic. Still, as always, E came through like a politician during election time. With a little financial expertise, his trusty broker made it happen. As Eric

walked through the foyer into the plush and majestic living room, the two briefcases he carried symbolized his dependability.

"What's happening, baby boy?" The aroma from the food wafted through the air. E paused and savored the smell.

"That shit smells good. That's your work?" he asked, making small talk but seeing the turmoil Dre's life was in on his face.

"E-Mo, on the real, I'm ready for this shit to be over. This is all my fault. First, I should've never stuck my dick in that bitch, knowing I didn't want her. Then, I didn't take heed to your warnings and underestimated that nigga. But, on everything I love, when I find him, he's a dead muthafucka! That's my word!"

"Yeah, I feel you, homie," E said. "Let's get Dee back first. We'll cross that other bridge when we get there. Right now let's see what you working with. I'm starving." They went into the kitchen.

Within the hour, everyone had arrived. Lucky, A.D. and Future listened to the plans, understanding that it was critical for someone to be at the two McDonald's locations waiting for Dee Dee.

Tony told them about the investigation unfolding around him and that Monica was the informant.

"Tony, maybe you ought to lay low on this one. I think we can handle it," Dre said.

Tony's eyes narrowed as he stood in the middle of

the kitchen. "Nah, nigga, fuck that. I'm going tonight, I don't give a fuck about that job or anything else. My only concern is getting my woman back!" Tony was zoned out and needed to release his frustrations. "Yo Dre, I swear if he put one hand on her, I swear, I'll hunt that nigga down and blow his muthafuckin' brains out myself!" He intercepted the Optimo being passed around and took a long, deep pull on the hydroponic weed.

Amazed, everyone looked on. His eyes were blood-shot and veins covered his forehead.

Seated on a stool, he looked up at them and started laughing. "What the fuck ya'll looking at?" He glanced at the blunt in his hand. "And what ya'll got in that shit? This ain't no ordinary blow."

After this episode with Tony, no one could deny his participation. As the afternoon came and went, they recounted the cash. Just as requested, there was ten million dollars in all. Each briefcase held 500 ten-thousand-dollar stacks. No one in the room had ever seen such a stupendous amount of money at one time. Nonetheless, there was no procrastination. They gladly handed it over in order to bring a loved one home safely.

There were two McDonald's restaurants in close proximity to the designated drop spot. Two hours prior to the scheduled time, both were covered. With binoc-

ulars and weapons, Tony and Future sat incognito in Tony's Navigator across the street from the first restaurant. A.D. drove the Cadillac STS while Lucky rode shotgun, covering the other one. Dre and E sat waiting for the drop time at a BBQ joint a few miles away.

"You all right?" E asked.

"I'm cool, E-Mo. I just wish we could see Dee Dee before we drop the money. There's too much cushion."

"It ain't a whole lot we can do about that. What you gon' do, not pay the nigga?"

Dre pondered. "Yeah, I know. I wish we could somehow, some way, get the drop on dude."

"I do too, but I doubt if he's even here," E thought out loud.

"Shiitt! That ain't no few dollars. Nigga, that's ten muthafuckin' million. That nigga somewhere watching. You can bet that," Dre rationalized.

"You right," E said, glancing at his Rolex Presidential. "It's about that time, partna."

Dre cruised down Kedzie Street past A.D. and Lucky. He wanted to make sure they were in place. E was in the back of the Range Rover. The rear seats were down, giving him a little room to stretch out. Dre was instructed to be alone, so as he turned the corner on Homan Avenue, he let the front windows down. He knew E was concealed in the back behind the tint and wanted to remove all doubts of being accompanied.

The warehouse came into view. Hesitantly, Dre drove toward the back entrance.

"You see anything?" E whispered.

"Nothing," he answered through clenched teeth.

He brought the truck to a halt and took a few deep breaths. Scanning the area for movement, he grabbed the two briefcases sitting on the passenger's seat.

"Well, here we go," he said as he opened the door and stepped out onto the frozen concrete. With every step he took, he expected to hear shots ring out. Yet, nothing happened. He got closer then stood in front of the door. He set the briefcases down and fought the urge to knock. No sound could be detected from the other side.

As he turned to walk away, he thought he heard what sounded like a door sliding open or closed. The anticipation of shots was even greater as he moved back toward the truck. *I should have backed this bitch in,* he thought.

Once inside the vehicle, he scurried for the phone to notify the others that he made the drop. When he pushed talk, he barely caught the door to the warehouse opening and a deft hand seizing the money.

"Somebody just took the money," Dre said as he put the truck in gear.

"Let's get the hell out of here then!" E said.

They both had a sense of alarm. Suddenly, they saw the plot clearly. Once the money was secure, they would

attempt to kill Dre.

A shot rang out, shattering the back passenger window, piercing the quiet of the night. The slight movement Dre made to look through the rear window saved his life. The bullet whisked past his head so close that a breeze could be felt and the sound rang in his ear.

"Oh, these niggas came to play!" Dre hollered as he ducked down and stepped on the gas. He sideswiped a garbage dumpster and sent E slamming against the opposite side of the truck.

The next bullet shattered the rear window, sending shards of glass down upon E. "Come on, D-Mo! Get us out of here! It's all on you, homie," E said as another shot rang out.

When it was over and done with, they made it out unharmed, but the Range Rover was a wreck. As they drove away from the point of ambush, they knew what they didn't want to acknowledge—they fell for the bullshit.

When Dre recovered the phone from the floorboard, Tony was still on the line. "Somebody say something, damnit!"

"Yeah, yeah, man ya'll got Dee Dee?" Dre asked.

"Nah, man. We ain't see shit! Where the hell is she?" Tony asked hysterically.

"Go back to the warehouse," E ordered.

Dre spun the truck 180 degrees and sped toward the warehouse. Seeing that there were no cars at the back

entrance, he drove to the front of the building. They turned the corner in time to see a Yukon fishtail around the opposite corner out of sight. The powerful engine of the Range Rover came to life as Dre floored it, but the pursuit was short-lived as the back tire blew out from the rubbing of the rear panel that rested on it. As the truck veered out of control, it came to rest wrapped around a light pole.

"Damnit!" Dre barked, slamming his hands on the dashboard.

"Ohh…shit…" He heard a groan from the back and turned around to check on E.

"Man, you all right?"

"I…ohh…think my ribs are broken," E said in obvious pain.

The others pulled up behind Dre and ran to the truck.

"Ya'll OK?"

"I'm good, but we need to get E to a hospital."

"I'll call a tow truck and meet ya'll there," Tony said.

"Nah, I'll meet you back at your crib," Dre said as Lucky and Future helped E get in A.D.'s Cadillac. Dre left for the hospital hoping his boy would be OK.

At St. Anthony's Hospital, Dre sat in A.D.'s Cadillac with his head hung low. He was waiting on Trina to arrive, to stay with E, so he could join the others at Tony's house. The recent, unsettling turn of events wore heavily on his mind. It was hard to be optimistic with

what and how things had transpired.

It was three o'clock in the morning when Trina pulled into the emergency room parking lot. He blew the horn to alert her of his whereabouts. She came and got in on the passenger side.

"How is he, DeAndre?"

"He's cool, just a few broken ribs. He should be fine. They were wrapping him when I stepped out."

"Well, what about you?" she asked. "I know you don't think the most of me, but I really do in some kind of strange way love E. Enough of that. What you need to know is that Dee Dee is depending on you. So don't give up. Something good will happen." She touched his arm.

"Thanks, Trina. I'm so twisted with the shit that just went down, I don't know what the fuck to do."

"Well, I know you won't give up."

"Oh, it's no question that I'm gonna use every resource available to bring her home... or die trying. Now let's go check on E," Dre said, getting out of the truck. Trina followed closely behind.

FIFTEEN

Thanksgiving came and went without so much as a piece of turkey for Dre, let alone a family to share it with. Other than life and Ebony, there wasn't much to be thankful for. Dre wanted to be hopeful, but he was pretty sure that Dee Dee was either hurt, dead or never coming back. After having taken such a tremendous loss, he fought the urge to pick up another package of dope. He knew from Tony that he was being watched, and lately, luck didn't seem to be on his side.

Already exceeding his expectations in the game, he didn't want to make things worse by falling to another federal bid. What he wanted was to get Dee Dee back, marry Ebony and be through with the game. There were very few winners, but even those who won the

battle by getting rich, lost the war. Dre had heard it been said, time and time again, that you'll either end up dead or in jail, but no one seemed to heed the warning even though the writing was between the brick walls that expanded daily. He detected a change in himself that had manifested in his recent trials and tribulations.

Glancing at the clock, in the darkness of his bedroom, he turned the radio on. The voice of Dr. Mutulu Shakur, a political prisoner at USP Atlanta and a brother in the struggle to obtain justice and equality for blacks and other minorities, boomed through the speakers. Dre gave Mutulu his undivided attention.

First, let me thank you for lending me your ear, giving me the opportunity to reason with you brothers and sisters. I want to establish one thing from the onset. I might say a few things that won't sit well with you; however, I believe it is important and needs to be said.

But, let's get one thing clear. I am not a hater. In fact, it's because of my love for you all, and the faith I have in you, that I will discuss the game, hustle and the underground economy.

Most of you that are out there hustling and making economic compensations know no other way than to fall into the conspired trap of US drug activity. Some will argue that you have alternatives. Today, that is not my issue or concern.

What we need to do is put the game in a historical context so that you can make a sound decision as to how you must approach the rest of your life.

It's no secret that in this game there are three known facts:You can get rich. You will go to jail. You will get killed. The game, as we know

it today, is dead. Yesterday's hustler was important in bringing a significant and somewhat predictable economic source into our community, and that gave us some financial self-determination. The numbers game and the drug game merged together, yet, at all times, there was an overriding objective. As contradictory as it may seem, our community, nation and vitality was the objective.

The skill derived from the flat foot hustle helped to shape an army of businessmen and women and create a financial system out of the eyes and ears of this government. Today, there are serious moral and financial issues with the so-called game, the hustle, street life, etc. The participants have no honor, and they have no principles. I know most of you join the life to accomplish goals of providing for your family, emerging as an entrepreneur, and uplifting your community. But the game sucks you right into the abyss of the decadent—money, power and sex—which is on par with the technically deprived brother and sister of Africa and Asia, who are killing each other at the behest of the enemy.

You ally yourself with the forces of outside influences. You were told about the CIA's collaboration with the California drug cartel. Gary Webb and Freeway Rick's indictment broke it down for you. Sister Maxine Waters traveled all over the country crying foul and we didn't take advantage of the game. That was the best chance for the big boys, playas and hustlers to play the game, streamline the hustle, get out of the hood, and enforce a thug code that wouldn't have turned the community and our nation into a destructive force.

See, it was your own lack of morals and principles that pushed our people into the arms of our enemy, begging them to lock you up for the rest of your natural life with the mandatory sentences.

In New York, Larry Davis told you. Hell, he showed you, that the police had him selling and fulfilling contracts on drug crews for the purpose of creating drug wars amongst each other, a standard COINTELPRO tactic. But no, you still didn't take heed.

In Chicago and throughout the Midwest, Larry Hoover tried to redirect the game and operations into a needed political machine, clearly bucking the political system. And look what happened where he's at.

You've sold and killed for the Arabs, Columbians, Cubans and Jamaicans and have rotted in jail because of betrayal. You've seen the RICO Laws and now, the domestic terrorist laws, snatch the life right out of any attempt to turn "bad" money into good business, showing you that it's not what you are, but who you are.

The most important thing is what this government wants to do to us, and if you all continue to play the game without conspiring to make things better for us all, then you as an individual will go the way of an animal or insect that eats on itself when it's wounded.

Before I close, let me say this, your survival is predicated on the government's powers to strategize on us as a people. You are not an island. A few of you will make it, but the majority will be sucked right back into the abyss of the game that is jail or death. We must draw a line in the sand on morals and principle and self-determination.

Now, I'm trying to give the game a lifesaver. I hope you swallow and digest it. Continue to search for the truth, aim high and go all out. Stiff resistance. Peace and love, brothers and sisters.

When Mutulu's speech was over Dre continued to lie in bed, still digesting his philosophy. It was as if, in some way, that message was meant specifically for him as messages usually come during the most troubling

and confusing times. It's just a matter of being quiet, and still, long enough to receive them. He was the wounded animal. He realized that the blueprint, which took five years of thinking in a federal penitentiary to develop, was scrapped in less than a year on the street—or even less so—within the three minutes of reasoning. He understood it was time for him to do better because he finally knew better. But he had one last mission to accomplish. And whether it be illegal or legal, it had to happen. He had to bring Dee Dee home.

For Dee Dee and her chance of survival, things had taken a drastic turn for the worse. Rich was already furious about her attempt to kill him, but after successfully extracting the money out of Dre's hands, he was rabid. There was no compassion in his actions or attitude. He became downright satanic, continuously perpetuating evil.

Days and nights seemed to have blended together for Dee Dee. She was moved to a different place but still didn't know her whereabouts. During the few days that Rich was gone, the wound on her head was healing, and she practically had to beg Nine to let her take a shower. She felt disgusting from wallowing in blood, sweat and cum. He gave in only after he had satisfied himself and came in her face one more time.

Rich's voice signaled his return. From the conversa-

tions she overheard, she knew Rich was on his way back out of town. She prayed for him to let her go, but it appeared unlikely. It was less than a week until Christmas, so Rich gave Nine his final instructions.

"If I come back and that backstabbing bitch's brains is blown out, I won't be upset," Rich said as he packed a small suitcase.

Nine peered at Dee Dee, who sat on the floor, motionless and broken. A glint of delight sparkled in his eyes. "Go ahead and take care of business. I'm gonna hold down the fort while you gone, you know that."

"Yeah, imagine that," Rich replied, understanding Nine's excitement.

Dee Dee looked in Rich's direction. "I know they paid the money you asked for, Rich. Why don't you let me go," she pleaded. "That's the least you can do, hold up your end of the deal."

Rich stopped packing and turned to face her. "Now the shoe is on the other foot and you want to bargain. Imagine that! But there wasn't no compromise or bargaining when you thought that nigga could protect you from me, was it Dee Dee? You made me do this. I called and gave you the opportunity for us to talk about things, but you weren't trying to hear that. It didn't matter that when I met you, when you barely had a change of clothes, let alone a decent ride or place to lay your head," he said as he approached her, sitting on the couch. The more he talked, the angrier he became. "For

more than five years, I took care of you! All you had to do was want something and you got it. And that's not to mention all the shit you probably stole. So don't talk to me about holding up my end of no damn deal. You crossed me, but it's gonna be a lifelong lesson; you'll see that my money ain't free." He grabbed a handful of her hair. "Look at me! I spend my money on what I fuck, drive and control. It ain't a whole lot to that."

As hard as Dee Dee tried not to cry, tears fell from her eyes. She wanted to kill him in the worst way, as being at his mercy and being helpless hurt her more than anything they could do or say to her.

Rich addressed Nine, giving him his final instructions before leaving. "I'm sure I'll be away until after the New Year, so it's all on you," he said, imitating shooting a gun while nodding in Dee Dee's direction. "You know how to reach me."

"Man, go 'head and take care of your business. I got this," Nine reassured him. "There won't be any problems whatsoever."

"I know it won't homie. Maybe you can come that way for New Year's, huh?"

"That's what I'm talking 'bout! You know the girls love the way Nine puts it down," he said, laughing and slapping his partna's hand.

"What other choice do we have?" Tony asked as he paced back and forth. "If we file a missing persons

report, it won't just be five or six of us trying to cover the whole Chicago area. As it is right now, we don't stand a chance."

They were at Dre and Ebony's house and the tension in the air was thick. "Don't nobody want Dee Dee back more than me, but I ain't involving no muthafuckin' cops, regardless what the fuck happens...even death," Dre said. "I understand what you're saying, but that's not how we do things, Tony. You knew what time it was before you got entangled in this game. And you know damn well the cops don't give a fuck 'bout no missing persons report!"

"Yeah, well, I disagree," Tony responded, feeling helpless.

"That's on you, but it ain't debatable, my man," Dre said, looking at Tony who stood with his arms crossed.

E got off the phone and turned his attention to them. "Let's just give it a few more days and see what happens. I got some people looking into something. D-Mo, have you heard from Monica?"

"I don't know where that bitch disappeared to," Dre answered. "I stopped by her spot last night and all her lights were off."

"I believe she can lead us to them niggas," E said.

Tony was in a far away place as he sat at the window. He didn't want to be the first to break the news. It would look too suspicious. They would find out sooner or later. Nobody really understood the length he was

willing to go to bring his woman home, not even Dre. That is if she wasn't already dead. "Hey, I'm gon' holla at ya'll later," he said as he got his bag and walked out of the door.

Ebony was entering the house as Tony was leaving. They almost collided. She spoke, "Hi, Tony."

Tony never broke stride, nor did he speak. He went straight to his car and sped off.

SIXTEEN

Ebony and Dre rarely disagreed, and argued even less. But Dee Dee's kidnapping had everybody's nerves on edge, so Dre refused to let things die as they took the two-hour commute to O'Hare Airport.

"Ebony, there's no logical reason you should be risking your life every day on a damn airplane," Dre roared. "I take enough risks for the you and me. Besides, I got plenty money to take care of us! You are *going* to quit that job today," he ordered.

"You need to remember who you're talking to because you seem to have me mixed up with one of your other whores," she said, raising her voice back at him. "I don't order you around, and I expect the same thing from you, DeAndre! What am I supposed to do

after I decide to quit my damn job? Sit in that big-ass house all by myself? That ain't happening! I'll give up my job when you give up those streets. Not before!"

Dre was incensed at not having his way. All his life, he controlled his women so he really didn't know how to handle this new situation. His knuckles were white from his grip on the steering wheel. The Kennedy Expressway was barren, and he pressed the pedal of the Viper to the floor. The speedometer disappeared after reading 140 mph.

Ebony sat scared in the passenger seat but unwilling to give him the satisfaction of knowing her emotional status. So, with her feet pressed firmly against the floorboard, she said nothing.

Dre was driving so fast he barely missed a stalled car on the side of the road. "Stop the car and let me out! Now!" she screamed.

"Where are you going at night, in the middle of nowhere?" he asked.

"Stop the car and let me out, DeAndre!" She opened the door.

She surprised him, so he reached out and grabbed her three-quarter-length chocolate colored mink coat and yanked her back toward him. Cautiously slowing the car down, he eased to the side of the road and parked.

"What the fuck is yo' problem?" he yelled as he held her by the collar of her coat.

"You!"

"Yo, I ain't got time for yo' shit, Ebony!"

"We can easily solve that problem, boo boo!"

"Is that a threat?"

"What you think?"

"Fuck you then! Take yo' ass on!" he barked, letting her go.

As soon as he released his hold on her, she turned and slapped the cowboy shit out of him. He touched his bottom lip then looked over at her with puppy dog eyes. "Don't ever put yo' hands on me again," she hissed as she jumped out of the car and started walking down the dark, predawn expressway.

He sat in shock, watching her, as the flow of blood dripped onto his lap. "Shit," he grumbled as he eased the car along behind her.

Seeing that she had no intention of stopping, he got out of the car and ran to catch up to her. He never thought he would be saying to any woman the words that he once equated with being soft and weak, but they spilled out of his mouth like Gerber peas out of a baby's. "I'm sorry," he said as he wrapped her in his arms. "This is getting the best of me. I can't stand the thought of losing you, too." He wiped the tears from her eyes.

"DeAndre, I feel your pain. We're in this together," she said as she allowed him to lead her back to the car. "I'm with you, I am, but that does not mean I'm gonna

let you order me around. I do have a mind of my own. Because I love you, I will always take into consideration the things you ask of me, and nine out of ten times, I will abide by your wishes, but I won't be ordered."

It wasn't a whole lot to say in response. She made it easy for him to understand and he respected it. "You're right, baby," he said, turning up the volume on the radio.

They continued the ride in silence as D'Angelo and Lauryn Hill sang about everything he was thinking. He made sure she understood as he cried out loud. "'Without you I'd go through withdrawal…with you it's never either or…nothing even matters, if I'm not wit' you."

Ebony sat in the flight attendant section of the plane while her co-worker made sure the first class passengers found their designated seats. All morning, she had been feeling nauseated, so she needed to rest for a while longer. She felt bad about parting with Dre on such a bad note. Maybe she overreacted, knowing the tremendous amount of stress he was under. Several times, she was tempted to pick up the phone and call him but she decided to wait until the plane was airborne.

She knew how he felt about her being away so much. Her resignation papers had been in for almost a week. Still, she didn't like to be ordered around, and his

commanding attitude made her rebel. She knew she could meet him halfway but didn't think it was wise to give in so early. She didn't want him to make it a habit of telling her what to do because she preferred he ask. She promised herself that she would make it up to him.

Observing the monitors, Ebony saw everyone was seated. Reluctantly, she headed for her section. She looked in on the pilots to update them. "Captain Summerlin, Mr. White, all passengers are present and seated."

Mr. White turned in his seat and looked at her from head to toe. His lust was shameless. Many nights, he had fucked his wife thinking about licking between her smooth, mocha legs. "Well, hello Ebony," he said, looking directly at her breasts.

"Excuse me, Mr. White, are you talking to me?" she asked with a slight grin on her face. He had been trying to fuck her for years.

"No, Ebony, I don't think he is," Captain Summerlin answered, laughing and admiring how well Ebony handled what could be construed as sexual harassment.

With a growing erection and a flushed face, Mr. White finally responded. "Actually, well, you know," he fought to get his words out. "Yes, I was talking to you, but you can't blame a man for looking, can you?"

"If you say so, Mr. White."

"Good then," he said. "We should be cleared for take off in the next three or four minutes."

"That's fine. I'll inform the passengers," she said as she turned to leave.

Their eyes followed Ebony as she walked out of the cockpit. Looking at her ass and big pretty legs, their thoughts were the same.

"I bet that's some good black pussy, Captain."

"You can say that again," Captain Summerlin replied, giving his co-pilot five.

Once they were cleared for take-off and the 747 sat waiting for its turn to trek down the runway, Ebony spoke into the intercom. "Good morning, ladies and gentlemen. Thank you for flying Continental Airlines. Your Chief Pilot is Captain Summerlin and Mr. White is co-pilot for this nonstop flight to Atlanta. The estimated time of arrival is 11:45. Keep in mind that we will travel through a time zone change and gain an hour, so be sure to move your watches up one hour. Be sure to leave your seatbelts fastened until the red light at the front of the plane goes off. My name is Ebony, feel free to use your intercom call button should you need me for anything. Thank you once again for using Continental Airlines as your choice for travel."

As the plane began its descent down the runway, she found her seat and fastened her seatbelt. She thought about Dre, her love for him and how much she needed to hear his voice. *Once we level out, I'll call him*, she reasoned.

♦ ♦ ♦

As Rich sat in the first class section of the plane, he

listened to the sweet and sexy voice of the flight attendant. Although she had such a nasty attitude the last time they met, she would make his trip more interesting and a lot quicker.

The effect of the cocaine he was snorting was intense. He had a serious hard-on and thought it would be a good time to fulfill one of his biggest fantasies. He pressed the intercom.

He watched Ebony as she stepped through the front partition. As she drew nearer, a smile spread across his face.

Ebony was aggravated that someone summoned her so soon into the flight. *I need to handle this quickly*, she thought. At the sight of him, the phony smile on her face was replaced with a frown of uneasiness. Nervousness permeated her, but she played it off smoothly.

"Good morning, sir. May I help you?" she asked, with her hands clasped behind her back to conceal their tremble.

"Hello, beautiful," Rich said, smiling. "This must be a sign, us meeting like this again. Have you considered my previous offer of us spending some time together?"

"Well, I must say that this is a coincidence, but like I said before, I'm engaged. Even if I wasn't, I wouldn't go out with someone whose name I didn't know," she responded as her heart thundered in her chest, and her mind formulated a course of action.

"Save the games, Ebony. I'm sure you've checked the manifest."

"As a matter of fact, I didn't. This is my first time seeing you. As long as a passenger isn't a terrorist, I could care less about a name. Besides, people fly under aliases all the time."

"I like you. Not only are you beautiful, but smart, too," he said as he wiped drug induced sweat from his brow. "My name is Rich. Now once this plane lands can I take you out?"

Ebony gave him a sexy smile as she put her hand on her hip. "My, don't we move fast? Didn't I tell you that I was engaged? What would my fiancé say?"

"How would he know? I never kiss and tell, baby."

"Well, that's good to know," she said, a brief glimmer of hatred seeping past the act that she was putting on. "How about if I get you a drink and think about your proposition?"

"You do that, and don't be too long. I hate waiting," he said, putting his hand in between his legs, adjusting his dick so that its erect state was obvious.

♦ ♦ ♦

For a moment, Ebony didn't think Dre would answer the phone before she heard his groggy voice. "Hello?" he said.

"Baby."

"What is it, Ebony?" he asked, becoming alarmed by the tone of her voice.

"He's on the plane with me," she whispered as though Rich was listening to her.

"Who is on the plane with you?" He was fully awake now.

"Rich! He's on the plane as we speak."

The seconds of silence that filled the line seemed to last forever. He was unsure how she would react to his next suggestion while she was anticipating his request, knowing what he was thinking. "Listen, baby girl, I wouldn't ask this of you if it wasn't extremely important, but you're our only hope. Do you understand?"

"Yes, I understand, DeAndre," she answered. "But what do you want me to do?"

"I want you to do whatever it takes to find out where he's going and where he'll be staying. Try to keep him in your sight until I can get there!"

"Dre, you can't get here in time. He's on a connecting flight out of Atlanta to the Caribbean at 3 o'clock."

"Ebony, you've got to think of something. Flirt with the nigga or something. You've got to hold him, some kind of way, until I can get there. I'm out on the first thing smoking, baby."

"You aren't listening to me, DeAndre!" Ebony wanted to be sure he understood what he was telling her to do. "Are you aware that this maniac ain't trying to flirt, he's trying to fuck me. Do you understand that?"

"Yeah, I do, and I'll call you as soon as I get there. But I need you to try your best to keep him there, OK?"

"DeAndre." She whispered his name.

"Yes, baby?"

"Do you love me?"

"With all my heart and soul, Mrs. Smith."

"I don't think it's possible to love you more than I love you right now, baby. You are the best thing that happened to me and without you, I'm nothing." Ebony tried to take a deep breath but choked. "Will you please hurry up?" she asked through her sobs.

"I'll call you from the airport in Atlanta, or you call me if you need me."

"See you soon," she said as she hung up the phone.

SEVENTEEN

Ebony stood just inside the flight attendant section, trying to calm down and restore her heartbeat to its normal rate. She had never been placed on center stage, where her performance meant so much to so many people. She wiped her sweaty palms on the front of her skirt and took the first step. She made a quick round to make sure the passengers were comfortable. Other than a few requests, everyone except Rich was fine. He hit his call button again.

Ebony mustered a smile as she reached his seat. "Yes, may I help you, Rich?"

"It all depends if it can be personal and not professional," he said.

"One thing about you, you are persistent."

He noticed that she was a little looser than previously. He gave it his best shot. "Ebony, tell me, are we going to spend some time together or what?"

"That depends on if you promise not to tell my fiancé, and if you can find the time," she responded, teasingly.

"You got my word on that, beautiful lady," he said, somewhat surprised that it had been so easy.

A blind passenger called, needing to be assisted to the bathroom. "I'll be back," she assured Rich. His dick got harder as watched Ebony assist the passenger.

As she helped the woman return to her seat, she decided she would use the bathroom as well. Watching her walk toward the lavatory again, a devious thought came to his mind and he followed her.

As she tried to close the door, two arms appeared then a full body before she was able to turn the latch on the door. Locking it behind him, his arms engulfed her from behind. His dick pressed against her ass and he kissed her on the neck. "What a coincidence."

"You're not supposed to be in here," she warned him.

"No one knows I'm in here but me and you. And like I said before, I don't kiss and tell." He spun her around and tried to put his hand between her legs.

"No, Rich. We can't do this in here. We will have plenty of time later," she said, surprised and angry at his overbearing personality.

"I'm sure you know that people do this all the time," he said as he picked her up and placed her on the sink. Standing in between her legs, he maneuvered her skirt up around her waist.

How she got in this situation was beyond her, but his hands were inside her G-string. "Rich!" She tried to stop him. "Rich, let's wait until we land and go somewhere to be alone."

He was hearing nothing as he continued to struggle with her.

Knock...Knock...Knock...

"Hello, is anyone in there?" a voice on the other side of the door called.

Rich was so preoccupied with trying to fuck Ebony that he'd forgotten that he was some twenty thousand feet up in the air. The knock scared him, and he quickly reached for his gun but felt nothing so when Ebony spoke, he actually heard what she was saying.

"Rich, this is my job. Don't do this. Let's get a hotel when we land." She closed her legs and jumped off the sink.

"Hello, is everything all right in there?" the voice said again.

"Yes, everything is fine. I'll be out in a minute," Ebony said to get the passenger away from the door. Straightening her clothes, she turned to Rich. "Later," she whispered and gave him a sly smile as she walked out and resumed assisting passengers.

As she reflected on what had just transpired, Ebony remembered how exciting and fulfilling the experience was with DeAndre. This made her realize even more how unpleasant and embarrassing it was with this lunatic. She knew what he was capable of, so she needed to be extra careful. Had she been alone, she would have cried. Had this been a movie and she an actress, she would've never accepted the role.

Dre called the others on his way to Midway Airport, a smaller, metropolitan airport closer to the South Side of town that accommodated limited airlines. There was a 9:30 flight that was due to arrive in Atlanta at 2 p.m. Being pressed for time, he packed very little. He could buy whatever else he needed.

There were a lot of mid-morning commuters, and he barely made the flight. He was the last person to board the plane. Anxious and impatient, it seemed to DeAndre as though the plane was moving slowly, but he realized that even the speed of sound wasn't fast enough for him right now. He wondered if an hour would be enough time to reach Rich once he landed. He did not want Rich to get on that plane leaving Atlanta.

He knew that everything lay in Ebony's hands, so he was overcome with guilt, having placed her in such a dangerous situation. Although she was their last hope, he couldn't stand the thought of losing her. Eric and

Tony's flight was due in Atlanta fifty-five minutes behind Dre's. They would wait at the airport for the call. Everyone hoped that Ebony was wise enough to follow through, because they needed to apprehend Rich in an isolated area.

Ebony claimed a family emergency and found a replacement for the next assignment, an overnight flight out West. She spent the next hour or so trying to stall Rich until Dre could get there.

Rich wouldn't go for her ploy of getting to know each other over an afternoon lunch. He wanted to know her with her clothes off, so he chose the Holiday Inn, a short distance from Hartsfield-Jackson, for the quick rendezvous he had in mind.

In the lobby, he went into the bag he carried and gave her five hundred dollars to get the suite. There was no doubt that it was the ransom money.

"Hey, beautiful, why don't you get the room while I make a quick run to the men's room," Rich said, smiling like the Cheshire Cat.

"Anything you want, big daddy," she responded. His brief absence would give her time to call DeAndre. Luckily, no one was checking in at the desk, so she quickly approached the clerk then placed the money and her identification on the counter. She informed him that she needed a suite and the room number before he proceeded with the registration so she could inform her fiancé of her whereabouts before he got on

the plane, in a few minutes, and would have to turn his cell phone off. The clerk hesitated.

"I'm exhausted, sir, and will probably be sleep when he arrives," she continued. He entered some data into the computer and set the key card.

"Suite 967," he said.

"Thank you. Can you give my ID and a key card to my fiancé when he arrives?" she asked as she hurried to make the phone call before Rich returned.

While Rich was in a bathroom stall snorting a pile of cocaine, Ebony hid behind the soda machine, giving Dre the suite number. It was still an hour before his arrival time. Just as she hung up the phone, Rich stepped into view. He didn't see her at first and thought she was in the bathroom as well.

He was impatient as he shifted from foot to foot, waiting on her. When he turned his back, she stepped from behind the machine. "Are you waiting for me?"

"Are you ready?" he asked as he placed his arm around her, leading the way to the elevator.

In their suite, Rich took his shirt and shoes off immediately and went to fix them drinks. "What would you like, beautiful?"

"A glass of orange juice will be fine. I don't drink often," she informed him as she sat on the love seat.

"One glass of orange juice coming right up," he said, feeling the pills in his pocket. "Why don't you take some of those clothes off so I can see how beautiful you

really are?"

"I thought you said you wanted to spend the weekend with me. But now all you want is to have sex with me then fly off into the sky. Do you treat all of your women like this?" She was trying to buy some time.

"I have some important business to handle in the Virgin Islands, but I won't be gone long," he said as he handed her the glass. "We'll have plenty of time to spend together, so for now, let's make the best out of the time we have."

Her nervousness caused her throat to become dry. She took a big swallow of the juice, never tasting the crushed up ecstasy pill.

Twenty minutes passed, and he had her down to her lace thong and bra in between the sheets on the queen-sized bed. The pills caused her body temperature to rise and perspiration formed between her breasts.

"I can't wait to taste your sweet, juicy pussy. Ebony, can I taste you?" he asked as he slid her panties off.

"No-no-no-no I can't," she whimpered as he caressed her body.

"C'mon baby, let me taste you."

All of a sudden Ebony was spaced out and horny. She caught herself assisting him in removing her underwear. His tongue entered her and she grabbed his head. "Umm, that feels so good! But I shouldn't be doing this!" she yelled as she experienced multiple orgasms.

"Shh…just be quiet," he told her as he took off his

clothes. He lifted her off the bed and into his arms. She wrapped her legs around his waist as he pressed her against the wall with his hands cupping her ass.

Using the wall as leverage, he bounced her on his dick. She screamed in his ear and bit his neck. She was wetter than ever before as her juices ran down his leg. The sounds from her pussy filled the room as he repeatedly slammed her back into the wall.

Not wanting to cum, he released her and she slid to the floor. At that point, she knew he had put something in her drink but being high wouldn't stop her from accomplishing her mission. "Was that sweet enough, Rich?" she asked, approaching him where he sat at the table. From behind him, she ran her hands over his chest.

He pulled her around in front of him, pushing her between his legs. His dick was hard and pointed right in her face. "Ask me after you finish," he told her, putting his dick in her mouth. He held her head, forcing his dick to the back of her throat. He was aroused by her struggle to accept every inch. Even when it seemed like she could take no more, he pushed farther. He dug deep into her mouth. Tears fell from her eyes as he increased his pace.

"Ahhh! Damn," he said as he came, holding her head down on his dick.

When he released her, she was no longer high but was humiliated and enraged. She went into the bath-

room where her tears flowed freely. It would be at least thirty more minutes before Dre would make it to her rescue.

When she came out of the bathroom, Rich was dressed.

"Where you going? I thought we was gon' spend some time together?"

"I would love to, beautiful, but I have some very important business that I must tend to. Why don't you come with me? You'll love it," he said, buckling his belt.

Daggers flew from her eyes. "I have a job to go to," she answered harshly. She wasn't going out of the states with him.

"Well, how about I send for you in the next day or so?" He took a card out of his wallet. "Call me when you're ready, OK?"

She glanced at her Cartier watch. *Fifteen more minutes*, she thought to herself. "I really would like that," she said, approaching him. "Can't you give me some more of that good dick before you run off?"

He attempted to button his pants. "Ebony, I gotta jet," he said, holding her hands. "We'll get together real soon. I promise." He then cupped her soft, bare ass.

She didn't know how much longer she could hold him off. "But baby, I need you right now! Just one more time, please," she begged, batting her hazel eyes at him.

"Damn, girl, you making my dick harder than muthafucka, but I gotta go. A nigga got things to take

care of. But I'll tell you what. Here, let me give you something for your troubles. Maybe, you can find you something nice while I'm gone." He opened the briefcase and took out one thousand dollars.

In the back of her mind, she couldn't believe that he was treating her like a prostitute, but the script didn't call for her to get offended. Sexily, she pouted as she approached him. "I want some more of this," she said as she squeezed his dick. "Not money."

"Trust me, babygirl, once I handle this you can have all the dick you want, but right now, I have to go." He broke her embrace, kissed her on the forehead and went out the door.

When the door closed she ran into the bathroom and threw up. She slid to the floor and cried. She felt extremely violated and immediately developed a personal vendetta against Rich. One day she would see him again, on her terms, and she vowed that it wouldn't be anything nice.

After calling Dre and finding out that his flight was delayed, she took a scalding hot shower and lay across the other undisturbed bed, waiting for him to get there.

EIGHTEEN

Rich was gone for more than two hours by the time Dre made it to Ebony. She was in bed, curled up in a fetal position, rocking back and forth when he entered the suite with the extra card left at the front desk. He scanned the room. Its disarray told part of the story while the tears, which came at the sight of him, told the rest.

Like a zombie, he walked toward her. "Are you all right?"

She wanted to say 'no,' but pulled herself together, nodding her head yes. She knew she didn't have to say what happened, nor was it the time. She sucked up the degradation she felt and showed him her strength and resiliency. "I'm going to be all right, DeAndre. I kept

him here as long as I could. He was in a hurry for some reason, but he left this," she said, giving him the card. "He wants me to come to him in the next few days."

"No, that's all right. We'll think of something else," he said as he went to the bar and poured a stiff drink.

"DeAndre, I want to go. I want to help bring Dee Dee back home. I mean it. I want to help." The look in her eyes disclosed her determination. "And I want to help you kill that bastard!"

"I'm gon' do that anyway, baby. I promise you that! What I can't promise is that I can save Dee Dee. It might be too late," he whispered as he picked the money up off the table.

The phone rang. Tony and Eric were on their way up. Ebony slipped on her skirt and blouse then greeted them with a smile. She was raised in an upper-class family but, somewhere along the perils of life, she inherited the mentality of someone who grew up in the inner city. Although the mindset rarely surfaced, it was available during times of need.

After she explained the entire encounter to them, omitting what happened in the room, they discussed their next course of action.

For them, Christmas Eve was spent inside of their hotel room, eating a long overdue, full-course meal. They ordered bottles of champagne and toasted to the days ahead.

"I wonder where that bitch Monica is at," Dre said,

eating a piece of a lamb chop.

E snapped his finger. It had almost slipped E's mind. "I knew I was forgetting something! They found Monica dead, strangled to death in her house early this morning."

"Get the fuck outta here!" Dre was shocked.

"Yep. No suspects, no motive, no nothing."

"One thing for sho', that devious-ass bitch deserved just what she got," Tony chimed in. "Yeah, that bitch had it coming!"

Tony's outburst was out of character, but nobody addressed the strange feeling that they had about Monica's death. It didn't matter. Instead, they discussed ways to trap Rich so they could locate Dee Dee.

"We know he's traveling without his sidekick," Dre stated. "Which leads me to believe that Nine is with Dee somewhere back home."

"So what are you saying?" Tony asked.

"What I'm saying is that somebody needs to be in Chicago to go get her because when I get my hands on this nigga, he gon' come clean, believe that!"

"Do you think you can take this nigga by yourself, homie?" Eric asked. "We don't know who he's with in the Caribbean."

"Whoever he with, they won't be there while he trying to get his rocks off," Dre said, glancing at Ebony who had fallen asleep across the bed.

E followed Dre's glance. "That nigga was in this

room," he said under his breath.

"Yeah, alone with my muthafuckin' wife!" Dre made sure his partna fully understood what had occurred.

"Let Tony go back to meet Future and the rest of them. I'm going with you. I want a piece of this nigga, too!"

"Don't think that I don't, but I do need to be close to Dee Dee when it comes time to bring her home," Tony added.

"We don't want you in any more trouble at work than you are already. It wouldn't look too good to be seen with me," Dre reminded.

"We don't have to worry about that because I got fired. They wanted to use me as a part of the investigation on you, so when I attempted to resign, they fired me."

"Man, don't even trip. When this is over I'm gon' make sure you straight," E said.

Nine had been trying to get Dee Dee to talk for the last couple of days, yet she said nothing. Instead, she just stared through him. She was in shock and began to hallucinate from the countless number of sleepless days and nights. He had raped her repeatedly. It no longer mattered what her fate was to be…she was ready to die. Her only wish was for Nine and Rich to die with her.

She looked toward her captor and saw someone else,

her father. Her beautiful smile had diminished as her already-full lips were swollen and disfigured, but she smiled nonetheless.

Perplexed at her expression, Nine watched Dee Dee. "What the fuck you smiling at?" He called her name repeatedly, but she never acknowledged him. He walked toward her. "Bitch, I know you hear me talking to you!" He stood in front of her as she continued to smile. She laughed as he grabbed her bruised arm. "OK, so you wanna play, huh?" Nine took the lit cigarette from his mouth and pressed it against her arm's bare skin.

Dee Dee didn't wince or utter a single word. Nothing he did to her could hurt her. She was beyond feeling. Even as the urine ran down her leg, she sat staring into the empty depths of nothing.

He threw her to the floor. Her breasts bounced and legs opened as easily as a rag doll as she lay on her back. The smile on her face continued to piss him off. Looking at her pussy, his dick sprang to life again, so he was ready to assault her one more time.

"Bitch, you want some of this again, don't you?" he asked, pulling down his pants in a hurry to free his dick.

She continued to smile at her own memories and didn't flinch when Nine grabbed her legs and spread them the length of his long arms.

Her pussy was dry but Nine thrust himself in her. *Hell, pussy is pussy*, he said to himself as she was able to

accommodate his nine-inch dick with no problem. Still, she didn't move nor react to his violent ramming. He became angered at her non-responsiveness, but it excited him even more. He grabbed Dee Dee's breasts hard, pulling and kneading them like dough to make her body meet his thrusts. Feeling the tingle in his balls, he grabbed her bottom lip and chin, stretching her mouth open. Pumping harder, Nine began to sweat. It dripped onto Dee Dee's face. Upon the brink of his orgasm, Nine spat in her mouth repeatedly. As he came inside of her, he grunted and pumped himself until his pipe was completely drained. When he was finished, he stood up. His dick was dripping with his remnants and her pussy was glistening from his semen. He became angry. "Kiss my ass!" he said as he shook his head in disgust. *What a Christmas Eve*, he thought as he picked up the phone to call Rich. He wanted to reconfirm their plans for the New Year and receive instructions on where to dispose of Dee Dee's body. The game was getting boring, and he was tired of being cooped up in a crib with a crazy bitch.

In Tony's den, Lucky, Future, A.D. and Lil Greg sat watching the Christmas Day football games while Cassandra, Shay, Pam and Charlene slaved in the kitchen, in attempt to bring the holiday spirit into Tony's home. There wasn't a whole lot to talk about, as well as no presents to exchange. Everybody wanted the

same thing.

Shay came into the room with an appetizer and some drinks. She spent some time in New Orleans while attending Dillard University, so the crawfish and beer attested to her Cajun side.

"Tony, your house is beautiful," she said. "And your kitchen is so nice and neat, everything is so easy to find."

"Thanks, Shay. Believe me, it's not my doing," Tony replied.

"Oh, trust me, I know. It's something about men and tidiness that just don't go together. Ain't that right, Future?" He didn't hear a word she said. "That proves my point." She pushed Future's head as she went back into the kitchen.

"Huh? What's up, baby?" Future asked. He looked at Tony. "Man, what was that all about?"

Tony's mind was in a far away place, hoping and wishing Dee Dee was still alive. He needed the one woman that made everything else seem so unimportant. He still remembered the words Dee Dee spoke to him in her living room not too long ago—*leave well enough alone*. But they were meaningless back then and even more so now. He didn't regret anything about that fateful morning on the lakefront, except that he let her out of his sight. And for once in his life, he understood a junkie's craving for a hit because he was fienin' for her.

Future stared at Tony, realizing that he had not heard him and was in a troubled state. "Tony," he called out, cutting off his deep thoughts.

Tony looked up and rubbed his hands over his face. "What was that you said?"

"It was nothing. I just want you to know that it's gon' be all right. We are close to breaking this thing open. She's gonna be all right," he said, knowing where Tony's thoughts were.

"Man, you just don't know how much I hope that's the case!"

Dre, Ebony and Eric celebrated Christmas in the hotel as well, but spent a small fortune shopping at Lenox Mall the day after. Ebony took them into what seemed like every store, buying clothes and other miscellaneous things. The shopaholics were in rare form as they covered the mall searching for sales. That served as a welcomed distraction. They went to Chops, a nice restaurant on East Paces Ferry to eat dinner. From there, they attended a poetry slam at the Apache Cafe before retiring back to their room late in the evening.

E had some contacts in Decatur, a town on the outskirts of the city, and he was to meet with them to acquire the necessary weapons. Ebony would see that they made it on the plane undetected, using her security clearance.

With E gone, they settled down and placed a phone

call to Rich to establish the day and time she would meet with him again. She became jittery, biting her lip and squeezing DeAndre's hand as the phone started ringing.

"Take it easy, baby," he said, soothing her. "It's gon' be all right."

She tried to calm down, but it was useless. Rich answered on the first ring. "Hello?" Music blasted in the background.

"Hello," Ebony responded on cue. "May I speak to Rich?"

"If this is who I think it is, you can do more than speak, beautiful. You can join me," he replied. "I wish you were here to put these island girls to shame. I used to think they were the best until I met you."

"I'm glad I left such a lasting impression," Ebony said, reaching for Dre's hand to put it under the chiffon BCBG skirt that he purchased for her. "My pussy is so wet!" She spoke the words into the phone, but they were meant for DeAndre, and he knew it. "I need you." She stood up and stepped out of her skirt.

Rich was enthused by her desire. "What exactly do you want from me?" he asked.

She began to undress him. "I want to suck your dick. Can I?" she asked Dre, bringing him in front of her.

"That sounds like a winner to me, beautiful. Why don't you catch a flight out tomorrow?"

"I'll be there." She took DeAndre into her mouth. "Mmmmm…I can't wait to make you cum."

"I can't either. Call me from the airport in St. Croix. I'll be waiting for you."

"OK. Bye, Rich," she said, disconnecting the line. She looked into Dre's eyes and saw the pain. "Make love to me."

"In any and every way you want me to," he replied as he slid her top over her head. Laying her on the bed, he climbed on top of her and their bodies became one.

NINETEEN

On the flight to the Caribbean, Ebony sat apart from Dre and E in the business section. She didn't want to draw any suspicion to them, nor the briefcase she carried. Conservatively dressed in a navy blue suit and moderate heels, she looked like a high-priced attorney on a business trip.

Dre and Eric, looking like typical vacationers, were dressed down in slacks and loafers. There was not a trace of their millionaire status as they flew coach.

In case they needed to make a switch with Ebony, an identical briefcase sat between them. But they didn't want to make things harder than they already were. It was going to be difficult enough putting a tail on Rich once he picked her up. Hopefully she would get the

opportunity to call and give them her exact location. They purchased a map of St. Croix for safekeeping.

They had spoken to the crew back home to put them on point, ready to strike. It wasn't a question of them getting Rich to talk once he was in their presence because this time there would be no chance at retaliation. None whatsoever.

As the plane started its descent from twenty thousand feet, the view was spectacular. The bluish-green water of the Caribbean Sea was mesmerizing. The sea shone like glass and the sand on the beach was unbelievably white. They both agreed that they would come back to visit one day, when this was all over.

Dre and E exited the plane ahead of Ebony. Rohlsen Airport was on jam because of the holiday season. They quickly made their way through the cluster of travelers to the phones where she would call Rich.

Ebony never looked their way as she used the phone that they left available for her. She set the briefcase next to the one they carried and dialed the number. She spoke loud enough for them to hear.

Learning that he would meet her at the racetrack across the street, Eric picked up Ebony's briefcase and retreated to the car rental desk, where Dre was filling out paperwork for their reserved vehicle.

At the racetrack, Dre and E nursed their non-alcoholic drinks as they observed Ebony across the room. It

wasn't long before they laid eyes on Rich for the first time since that drama-filled Fourth of July afternoon on the lakefront. He was dressed in white linen with red Mauri alligator sandals, and the diamonds on the sides of his Versace sunglasses sparkled. He approached her and wrapped his arms around her body in a close and intimate embrace, kissing her flush on the lips. Dre's whole body tensed at the sight of Rich kissing his woman. When Rich's hand slid down across her ass, Dre gulped his drink.

"I'm gon' kill that bitch-ass nigga, homie! On everything I love," he said as they moved closer to the exit doors.

They watched Ebony and Rich as the two went to place a bet on the next race. Ebony gave a stellar performance as she clung to Rich's arm, watching the race live on the television screen. She jumped up and down, cheering on their picks. When their trifecta came through, she jumped into his arms, kissing him.

After cashing in the winning ticket, they lingered for a while longer before heading toward the exit. When Dre and E saw them coming their way, they left out the door in front of them.

Thinking ahead, they parked the rental car close to the only exit, knowing that Rich would have to come out of that door when he left with Ebony. When he passed them, they followed at a safe distance.

Keeping Rich and Ebony in their sight was more dif-

ficult than Dre anticipated since he wasn't accustomed to driving on the left side of the street. Dre often lost sight of them but found them numerous times before eventually losing them completely.

"Do you see them, E-Mo?"

Eric was up in his seat, looking up and down the passing side streets. He caught a glimpse of the car down one of the streets as Dre flew past. "I think I just saw them going down that road back there!"

Dre slammed on the brakes in the bumper-to-bumper traffic, almost causing a major catastrophe as the cars behind narrowly missed his rear-end. "Shit!" Dre was furious. "These muthafuckas are a decade behind time," he said as he pulled to the side of the road, trying to figure out how to get back to the street they had just passed.

"Calm down, partna. Everything is gon' work out," E told him. "Ebony will get in touch with us."

Ebony knew that Dre and E were in a rental, but she didn't know the make, model or color of the car. She chanced a few glances in the side mirror, hoping to spot them but didn't.

She was pretty confident that she would get the opportunity to call once they arrived at Rich's destination.

She leaned toward Rich, her hand sliding up under his shirt, rubbing his bare chest. "Where are we going,

big daddy? I'm ready to be alone with you. This is going to be a night to remember. I'm going to blow your mind," she purred, really wanting to say, "blow your brains out."

"We have a wonderful night planned. I have another friend that I want you to meet. She's going to be joining us. She's bi-sexual, very sexy and dying to meet you. You feel what I'm saying?" he asked, running his hand up her smooth thighs.

"I don't know about that, Rich. I thought we would be spending time alone. Besides, I'm not into women."

The smile on Rich's face vanished in thin air, replaced with a scowl. "Don't knock it until you try it. I'm just trying to bring a little spontaneity into this thing, ma."

Ebony smiled. "I can be as spontaneous as you want me to be. Why should I have to share you with another woman?"

"You aren't sharing me with anyone, I'm sharing you. You know, just a lil' fun and games," he said, adjusting the temperature in the car. A quick glance between her legs revealed white lace panties. "After all, ain't that what an affair is supposed to be – new, different and exciting?"

"You make it sound wonderful."

"It will be. I promise." He smiled. "The beginning of something special."

On the contrary, she was thinking the end of some-

thing, or better yet, someone. He was disgusting and had a blatant disregard for humanity. He thought he ruled the world and everything in it. The more she was around him, the more she wanted to see him dead, and that hunger pushed her onward, dictating her next words. "I told you before that you are persistent. How can I say no?"

"That's just it, beautiful, you can't," he said as he pulled the car in front a stunning tropical home.

"I guess a ménage à trios it is." She pouted in a sexy way. "You know I wouldn't do this for no one else but you. I hope she's beautiful."

"She's gorgeous, but she ain't got shit on you." He grabbed her breast hard in anticipation of what was to come. She squirmed.

When he was gone, she hit the memory button on her phone to call Dre. Hearing his voice, she held the phone down below the window to lower the risk of being seen. As she spoke to him, she nodded her head like she was listening to the music.

Time only allowed for her to ease their minds, let them know that she wasn't stationary yet and to inform them that she would call back as soon as they touched down. Dre's voice, shouting a hundred questions, went unheard.

Ebony wasn't downright against a threesome but hated to be controlled. However, she had to admit that

the girl was indeed gorgeous. As they entered the St. Croix by the Sea Hotel, she wasn't any more against what she was about to do with the girl than with Rich by himself.

From the moment they entered Suite 769, he became a dictator who rivaled Hitler. He ordered them around, without the slightest doubt that they might resist. All the while, there was the hint of severe repercussion if they denied him. He emptied a pile of cocaine on the nightstand, took off his shirt and shoes and kicked back in the bed like the king he thought himself to be.

"Beautiful, why don't you and Rosalyn join me? But first, take off your clothes," he ordered them, while snorting a heap of the cocaine.

Ebony made her first crucial mistake. "Big daddy, I need to make a quick phone call to let my mother know that I made it safely," she said reaching for the phone and attempting to dial a number.

Rich's stare was unnerving and cold as January in Chicago. "Don't even think about it. Haven't you realized I'm a very impatient person?" He then pulled the phone out of her hand. "As a matter of fact, let's save the phone calls until this rendezvous is over." He snatched the hotel phone line out of the wall. "Now, Rosalyn, show her how gorgeous you really are."

Rosalyn was black as a pearl with dreads piled high on her head. She was five feet with a well-defined ass,

perky breasts and a thing for Ebony from the beginning. She undressed herself slowly, then undressed Ebony, admiring each part of her body.

Ebony realized that she was trapped in this situation. There was no way she could escape to call Dre before submitting to Rich's freaky games, so she relaxed and began to enjoy the curious and unfamiliar caresses from Rosalyn. She allowed herself to be led to the bed where light, tender kisses were placed upon her mocha skin. Rosalyn's touch was soft and gentle and felt good.

Rich managed to leave the powder alone long enough to finish undressing. He got a full bottle of Rémy from the bar. As he sipped from the bottle, he stroked his dick while becoming aroused by the contrast of Rosalyn's pink pussy and her jet-black skin as she leaned over the bed, eating Ebony out.

Ebony came twice before she moved her from in between her legs. She let Rosalyn kiss her as she looked at Rich. "Did you enjoy that, big daddy?"

"Of course I did." He handed them both a drink.

She remembered the last drink he gave her and she tried to decline his offer. "I think I'll pass this time. I want to remember this night."

"Stop acting like a stuck-up bitch and let the fuck go," he said as the alcohol and cocaine took effect on him. "You're starting to get on my muthafuckin' nerves with that good girl role you keep playin'! You better get wit it. You wouldn't like me if I got upset." He sneered

at her. "Now, let's toast to a night of ecstasy."

They touched glasses and Ebony faked a sip from her glass. The drugs and alcohol, along with her reluctance to swallow the laced drink, were enough to send him spiraling into a deadly state of anger.

She never saw the hand coming as it landed across the side of her face. "Bitch, you think you slick! Where I'm from, when we toast, we down our drink. Don't play games with me! Drink up so you can return Rosalyn's favor. I want to see how good you can eat some pussy," he said as he starting laughing.

Rosalyn was finished with her drink so she lay back on the bed, fingering herself while watching Ebony. She felt sorry for her, but was glad that Rich wasn't upset with her. "Come on, ma. It's going to be fun," she said as she guided Ebony between her legs.

Ebony finished her drink and started kissing the inside of her thighs. Her pussy was pink and moist with a naturally pleasant smell. She felt the first signs of the pill as she stuck her tongue inside Rosalyn's vagina.

"Yeah, that's what I'm talking about, beautiful," Rich said as he reached into the nightstand drawer. With the lubricating gel in his hand, he stood behind Ebony and slapped her hard on the ass. "See, it ain't as bad as you thought, is it?" He rubbed the cold, wet cream up and down the crack of her ass.

Ebony was high and getting into pleasing Rosalyn. She knew what felt good to her so she hit the same

spots. But the cold cream distracted her and she stopped. "Rich, don't do that," she said, turning her ass away from him.

"What the fuck did I tell you?" He snatched her by the hair. "Don't tell me what to do," he said as he pushed her head into the mattress. "You better learn to do less talking and more listening!" Placing his forearm at the back of her neck, he pinned her down and penetrated her asshole.

Ebony gritted her teeth as he fucked her violently. "You're hurting me! Please don't do this," she begged, turning her head from side to side.

"Shut up, bitch!" Sweat ran down his face as he worked his way to an intense orgasm. Once he was finished, he pushed her away from him and went into the bathroom.

Ebony lay, in excruciating pain, on the bed as tears streamed down her face. Rosalyn wiped them, trying to soothe her. "He is a very evil man," she said. "The same thing he do to you, he does to me."

"Why do you keep coming around then?" Ebony asked.

"He said that he would kill my family if I ever disobeyed him."

An idea came to her. "Listen Rosalyn, don't you want to be rid of this monster once and for all?" She nodded her head. "Good, because I have some friends that are looking for him, and I need you to go call them

for me, OK?"

"I'm sorry, but I can't. He will kill me and my family," she said, hysterically.

"No, he won't," she hissed. "After you make the phone call, leave and go home. You won't have to ever worry about him bothering you again." She gave her the number and two hundred dollars. "You have to call that number! It's important, Rosalyn! Tell whoever answers that I am at the St. Croix by the Sea Hotel in Suite 769. You have to do this! My life depends on it," Ebony insisted, stressing the importance of the call.

"OK, I will do it," Rosalyn agreed.

"Hurry! You have to go before he gets out of the shower," Ebony demanded, practically pushing her out of the door.

TWENTY

Dre paced up and down the harbor waiting on Ebony to call back. After so much time had elapsed, he feared the worst. "Maybe he found out somehow," he said to E. "They should have been wherever the fuck they were going by now!"

Eric was worried, too, but somebody needed to stay calm and Dre wasn't a good candidate. "It's only been two hours," he said. "Give it some more time, Dre."

The ringing of the phone brought silence. Before it could ring a second time, Dre answered it. "Ebony, where are you?" he blurted out.

"Um...this isn't Ebony," the caller on the other end informed. "I'm calling for a girl who instructed me to call. She wanted me to tell you she's at St. Croix by the

Sea, Suite 769."

"Who is this?" Dre asked, as he and Eric rushed to the car.

"My name is not important, but you need to hurry because she's in trouble."

"Where the hell is—Hello, hello? Damn, she hung up!"

"Who the fuck was that?" E asked.

"Man, I don't know, but whoever she was said that Ebony is at the St. Croix by the Sea, Suite 769. Check the map and see where the fuck that is," Dre commanded as he pulled out into traffic.

Rich was furious when he came out of the shower and found Rosalyn gone. He checked under the bed and came up with expression of relief. He looked at Ebony then sent his attention and anger in her direction.

"Why didn't you tell me that she was leaving?" With nothing but a towel around his waist, he approached her.

"We can still have our own private party, Rich," she pleaded with him, backing into the corner. Her head was spinning, her legs wobbled and the ecstasy made her body weak.

Once he reached her, he slapped her to the ground. "The rules have changed. You disappoint me, beautiful," Rich snarled and grabbed her hair as the towel fell from his waist.

She knew she was in trouble. "Let me make it up to you, big daddy," she begged, reaching out for him. She took him into her mouth hoping to buy more time. *Where are Dre and E?* she thought to herself. She began to wonder if Rosalyn made the call.

Tears ran down her face as Rich rammed his dick down her throat. His hands were twisted in her hair, rendering her helpless to his assault. "Arrghh... Arrghh." She tried to speak but couldn't get the words out. Nothing she did—scratching him or trying to push him away—would make him stop. On the verge of cumming, Rich pumped her mouth like it was a pussy. Ebony tasted the salty substance beginning to shoot out of his dick. Desperate times called for desperate measures, so she clamped her jaws down. Blood shot inside her mouth.

Although his facial expression screamed, Rich's wail stayed suspended in his throat.

"Aahhhhhhhhhh! Aahhhhhhhhhhh! Bitch, I'm gon' kill you!" he roared as he slung her against the wall with one hand while holding his injured dick with the other. He started kicking her, but the pain was too unbearable as blood seeped between his fingers, dripping onto the sunflower colored carpet. He picked up the lamp and threw it. It hit her across the head.

Ebony knew that he was going to kill her so the first chance she got, she ran for the door. There was no time to worry about her nudity. She snatched the door open

and ran right into the arms of someone.

Her consciousness transformed into fright, shock then relief as she fainted when she felt the familiar arms around her body.

Dre and Eric were just getting off the elevator when they heard the agonizing wail. They broke into a trot and were posed with guns drawn, ready to kick the door in when Ebony rushed out, running for her life.

Thinking quickly, E dashed past them into the room where Rich stood in the middle of the floor, butt naked, with his underwear held to his crotch. "Bitch nigga, don't move!" Eric ordered as he closed the distance between them.

Rich didn't put it together at first, but when he saw Dre come in with Ebony in his arms, he knew that he had been set up. He also knew their reason for being there, though he didn't know all the details.

After Dre helped Ebony dress, he placed her across the bed and turned toward Rich. His eyes shot daggers of fire and his veins pumped the venom of a snake ready to strike. "Where is she, Rich?" He asked the question as he walked toward him, the pistol held tightly in his hand. Without thought, he brought it down viciously across his face. The blow knocked Rich to his knees.

Blood from the gash ran down his face. "Let's talk about this," he said. He was reduced to less than a frac-

tion of the man he appeared to be in the past, when he had the upper hand.

Dre shot him in the leg. "Nigga, we ain't got time to talk. My patience with you left with my money. I'm gonna ask you one more time. Where is Dee Dee?"

"Let's tie his ass up," E said as he went to get the tape out of the briefcase.

"Man, I'm gon bleed to death!" Rich spoke, horrified.

"Shut the fuck up, nigga!" Dre was ready to kill him right then and there.

Eric returned with the tape. "You gon' die regardless. It's just a matter of how it's going to be. Quick and painless, or slow and torturous," he said as he took long strips of the duct tape to bind his wrists.

"Hand me that," E said to Dre as he pointed to the floor.

Tossing the material to him, Eric gagged Rich with his bloody underwear.

Ebony woke up and all the pain she felt eased when she saw Rich positioned on the floor. A smile spread across her face. She picked up the phone, ran up to him and slammed it against his head, knocking him out. Just as she was about to hit him upside the head again, Dre grabbed her arm.

"Baby, it's OK, it's OK," he said, holding her tightly.

"I want to kill him myself," she said as tears streamed down her face.

They picked Rich up and threw him on the bed. His unconsciousness gave them all time to think.

"Hold up a minute," Dre said. "We can't kill this nigga yet. We need to find Dee." He slapped Rich and woke him back up. Rich tried to talk, but realized he couldn't.

"I got something for this nigga," E said, going into the briefcase again.

Eric returned with a box of Morton Salt and a switchblade. "OK, you ain't got a whole lot of time to tell no muthafuckin' lies, because my patience with you is shot. I need to know two things from you and each time you lie, I'm gon' slice your ass and season it."

Rich mumbled something under his breath. "Hold up. You got something to say? Let's see what you have to say now, bitch!"

E cut through Rich's flesh, drawing fresh blood. Once he poured the salt in the wound, they had to put a pillow over Rich's head. His scream was piercing and tormenting. E removed the pillow once the wailing subsided. "Don't you dare cry like a bitch now, you tough muthafucka! You ain't felt pain yet," E said, looking at Rich's mangled dick. "Guess what's next, nigga."

Rich shook his head from side to side, mumbling some indistinguishable words.

"You ready to talk then, nigga?" E asked. Rich nodded his head vigorously up and down. "Well, just for good measure, because I don't trust you." E covered his

head and poured some salt into the deep gnaw wounds around Rich's dick.

Once again, the sounds were so wrenching that Eric, Dre and Ebony cringed. It took Rich longer than before to calm down.

"Check this out. It's simple. I got two questions for you, and nigga, you better have the right answers." E removed the underwear from Rich's mouth. "The first question is, where is Dee Dee? The second is, where is my muthafuckin' money?"

Dre and Ebony stood back, letting E do his thing. Neither of them were sure they could control themselves, so they watched and anxiously waited for Rich to give the location. Once that was verified, it would be their turn.

Rich began to shiver and his eyes started to blink slowly. "Please help me," he said, looking at all the blood he lost.

"Answer the question, nigga!"

"Man, it's some money under the bed, if that's what you want," Rich said, actually trying to strike a deal to spare his life. "There's plenty where that came from."

"Answer the other question," E said, opening the switchblade. Rich had several wounds that were bleeding profusely. He had lost a lot of blood and his weakness could be heard in his voice.

"She's at an apartment on Garfield and Damen," Rich said, finally giving them the information they

wanted. "It's cold," Rich said in a meek voice, as his color rushed from his skin.

Dre could contain himself no longer. "What's the address, nigga?" he slapped Rich.

"5517 West Damen Avenue," he said, barely audible, fading in and out of consciousness.

♦ ♦ ♦

Everybody back in Chicago had been sitting around waiting for the phone to ring, so when the call finally came, they moved.

It was five of them, Tony, Future, Lucky, A.D. and Lil Greg. Lucky was designated to stay behind in case they needed reinforcements. So, the four headed for the given location.

The apartment sat in the middle of a run-down, rat-infested neighborhood. They rode around the back of the dwelling, wanting to enter from the rear but the stairway to the single tenant had rotted and collapsed. They had no choice but to use the front street entrance.

Tony led the way into the building, up the stairs. Everybody's guns were drawn. There was a faint noise coming from the other side of the door, but nobody could distinguish it. On the silent count of three, they kicked in the door and poured into the apartment like SWAT.

At the sight of the door flying open, Nine leaped from the couch for his pistol on the coffee table. The

first shot caught him in the side of his leg. Stumbling back, he tried to raise the gun, but the second shot from Tony's .40 caliber Glock knocked him to the floor.

Everyone scanned the room, looking for Dee Dee. "Check the other rooms," Tony instructed. "She's got to be somewhere." He barely spotted her, balled up in a corner behind a foldout bed. She was naked, broken and shaking violently.

"Here she is!" Tony called out as he rushed to her side. "Dee Dee, baby, it's me." He wrapped her in his arms, rocking her back and forth. "I'm here baby. I got you, I got you." He kissed her repeatedly, oblivious to the foul smell coming from her cold and naked body.

Everybody was stunned as they stood around, looking at Dee Dee's mental and physical state.

A tear fell from Tony's eye as he looked at Nine. Kissing Dee Dee one more time, he instructed, "Take her to the car. I got it from here." Future, A.D. and Lil Greg did as they were told.

Nine's body was still, except for his rapid, irregular heartbeat. His eyes watched Tony as he approached. He bit his lip, trying to withstand the pain from his wounds. "Go ahead and kill me you coward muthafucka," he said as Tony bent down beside him. Tony said nothing, just stared at him. "That's what I thought! And to think you five-o," Nine said with a cough rocking his body and blood oozing from his mouth. "Your bitch got more balls than you do."

"It's good to know that you ain't scared to die, you low life piece-of-shit, 'cause I ain't got a problem killing yo' ass. As a matter of fact, it makes my dick hard," Tony said.

"Ask your bitch how she like a hard dick," Nine spat back.

Not the one to argue, Tony emptied the entire clip into his head.

Tony joined the others in the truck as they headed south toward his crib. "Somebody give Dre and E a call."

"We already took care of that," Lil Greg said. He looked back at Tony, who was stroking Dee Dee's face. "You all right man?"

"I am now," Tony said, whispering something in Dee's ear.

Dre, Ebony and Eric were waiting on the word from back home. The minutes passing by were agonizing, like awaiting a verdict after closing statements. They still weren't relieved yet because they didn't know if Dee Dee was dead or alive.

They had to keep Rich alive by covering him with a blanket, not wanting him to go into shock and die because there was a chance they would have to extract more information from him. Besides, they wanted to know the pleasure of rocking him to sleep.

Ebony felt better since she had taken a long hot bath.

She prayed that they found Dee Dee alive and that Rich didn't die because she wanted to be the one to cause him to take his last breath and she knew just the method she would use.

The phone rang, one good time, before E held it to his ear, "Yeah?" He listened for a minute, then a big smile spread over his face. He looked at Dre and Ebony, who were paralyzed, waiting. "They found her, and she's alive!"

"Yes! Yes!" Dre yelled as he hugged Ebony and Eric.

E directed his attention back to the phone. "No, not yet," he informed Lil Greg. "But, you know this nigga about to get his. It's definitely his day. OK. One love, homie," he said as he hung up the phone.

Ebony already had the switchblade in her hand. "Let me be the bitch that put this punk muthafucka to sleep!" She walked over to Rich and sliced him across his face. "Guess what, Bitch. You won't like me when I'm mad, either," she said as she grabbed a hold of his dick. His eyes got wide, and he opened his mouth, but words abandoned him. He shook his head vigorously. "I promise that you fucked with your last person today, nigga!" She pulled his dick toward her, and with one swift motion, she cut it off. Blood squirted everywhere as Rich screamed the screech of death. It was just a matter of time.

It was Dre's turn to finish him off. He stepped directly in front of him and aimed the automatic .45 at

his temple. "This one is for Dee Dee," he said as he pulled the trigger. "This one is for my dead homie, nigga!" He shot him a second time. "And this one is for me, my woman and my partnas who couldn't be here to put a bullet in you." He unloaded the gun into Rich's body. "You can stick a fork in that nigga," said Dre as he looked at the body. "Let's get outta here." They started gathering their things.

TWENTY-ONE

Their flight was scheduled for 9:30 a.m. New Year's Day, and they couldn't wait to get home. Everyone was ready to close this chapter of their lives. The past few days had been risky and strenuous, and as they pulled away from St. Croix by the Sea, neither of them dared to look back.

Dre and Eric made small talk while Ebony sat quietly in the back seat. He was worried about her, but he'd wait until they made it home to have her seen by a doctor.

With an hour to spare, they decided to spend it eating breakfast. Stix was a comfortable, cozy restaurant and the food smelled mouth-watering as they were seated.

Ebony's head was down, looking at the menu when the waitress came to take their order. She couldn't decide, so she let them order first.

"What will you be having, Miss?" the waitress asked.

"I'll have the boiled fish and fungi," Ebony said, looking up for the first time. When she saw Rosalyn standing at their table a smile began to slowly form on her face.

"Ebony!" Rosalyn said as they embraced.

"Rosalyn, thank you so much! You saved my life!"

Rosalyn's smile faded as she thought about Rich. "He's going to kill me."

"He won't be bothering you or anybody else, I promise."

"Excuse me. Could someone tell us what's going on?"

"Oh I'm sorry, baby. This is Rosalyn, the girl that called you for me."

They talked to Rosalyn until it was time to go. Dre noticed there was a special and intimate bond between them, but said nothing. He was glad that someone brought Ebony out of her state of depression.

As they got up to leave, Dre placed an envelope in Rosalyn's hand. "Just a small token of our appreciation," he said then walked out the door with Eric, leaving the two women alone. They held hands.

"Call me if you ever need anything," Ebony said.

"Anything?" Rosalyn smiled.

"That's right, anything," Ebony said, knowing what she meant. "Who knows, I might treat my husband to a double dose."

They stood, looking into each other's eyes. No words needed to be spoken. With a quick kiss on the lips, Ebony walked out the door.

They made one more stop by a local garbage dump, where they disposed of the bags in the trunk. Now, they were all set to go home.

The whole crew was at O'Hare, waiting when they exited the plane. Everybody was hugging and kissing, except Dee Dee. She stood off to the side with her arms wrapped tightly around herself.

Dre left the crowd and walked over to her. "How you doing, Dee?"

"I'm doing OK, DeAndre," she said, a slight smile on her face. "I was worried about you."

"Worried about me? Girl, stop playin'! I didn't know what I was going to do if you didn't make it back home."

Her smile disappeared quickly. "Where is he?"

"Thousands of miles away, rotting in a dumpster where he belongs."

"I heard what Ebony did. She's amazing, Dre. You better take good care of her!"

"Good care of who?" Ebony asked as she walked up.

She hugged Dee Dee. "Somebody better take care of me, because I can't stand any more pain." She looked at Dre.

"She ain't got nothing to worry about. She's tried and true," Dre responded.

Tony walked over to where they were. "Can I be a part of this tender moment?"

They opened their arms, welcoming Tony into their circle.

It was early evening when the convoy made its way toward the city. Dre was greeted with the many reminders of how precious life and freedom truly were.

They passed Mookie's house, and it had a "For Sale" sign in the yard. They also saw the entrance to Rich's North Side condo a short distance away. As they came into downtown Chicago, the Loop and MCC Chicago Federal Detention Center came into view. Seeing the FDC also brought about the not-so-long-ago feelings of despair that accompanied incarceration. Finally, they reached the South Side. Traffic slowed because of a funeral in progress. As they sat waiting, Monica's mother came through the funeral home doors, consumed with grief.

Dre bowed his head, saying a silent prayer for Monica, her family, and thanking God for his blessings despite all of the chances that they had taken.

Dee Dee had been home for over a week, and she

was getting better by the day. She almost resembled her old self as she moved throughout her home in Calumet City, packing. She and Tony were moving into their new home within a week and she couldn't wait to not be reminded of her old life. They were able to purchase an enormous house in Michigan City, Indiana, close to where Dre lived, with some of the money they recovered from Rich, the sale of both of their homes, the beauty salon and the special gift that Dre had been saving for her. She wanted to put a little more distance between herself and the ordeal she survived.

Tony walked into the room carrying a box. Dee Dee watched as he set it down. "What's up, baby? Why you looking at me like that?" he asked as he sat beside her.

Dee Dee put her arms around his neck and kissed him. "Because I love you, and I want to tell you how sorry I am."

"Sorry for what? There's nothing to be sorry about, Dee."

"Yes there is. When I met you, you were a police officer, living life without all the drama that came with being with me. You didn't deserve to go through all of this."

"Neither did you," he assured. "You didn't force me into anything. I came willingly, accepting all the consequences and I'd do it again, if that's what it'll take to have you for the rest of my life. That's what life's about, making the right choice and taking the best chance."

"And to think that I tried to dissuade you." She laughed. "I had to be the craziest woman in the world!"

"I won't hold that against you. I respect that you and your brother were cautious. Better safe than sorry," Tony said as he looked at the box on the floor. "What should I do with this?"

The box held memories of the many years she and Rich spent together. They had been everywhere and done everything, and the pictures in the box attested to the life they lived. Yet, she was never as happy as she was with Tony. She looked at him. "Burn that shit!"

◆ ◆ ◆

Dre sat at his desk in his home office, with stacks of money spread out everywhere. He and Eric were getting ready to invest. E was happy that his partna had finally taken his ability to negotiate, organize, distribute and collect and parlayed it into a legal business. That's what the come up is all about. Otherwise, it's meaningless. As Dre sat there counting the money, Mutulu's words kept creeping into his mind. *Very few will make it out of the game.*

He planned to be one of the few, knowing that if he continued on the path that he was on, he'd fall sooner or later. So, although he would always be a hustler, it was time to do some legit hustling. He just hoped it wasn't too late.

Dre knew he was at the crossroad of life, but he didn't realize that he had only one chance to make the

right choice.

Ring…Ring…

The phone broke his concentration. "Hello?"

"Dre, what's up?" There was a brief pause and a faint beeping sound in the background. "Hey man, check this out. I got a sweet deal up here on some of that boy. You trying to get in on this?" the caller said, his words being dictated by the agent who sat in the room with him. Dre recognized the voice. It was one of the dudes who sold dope for him when he first got out.

"Man, listen, don't call this house again with that bullshit!" Dre had a bad feeling. "You know that I ain't down with that type of activity. How did you get my muthafuckin' number, anyway?"

"Man, don't put the antennas up on me. You know I don't play no games. This is a once-in-a-lifetime deal. Can I count you in or what?"

"You haven't answered my question yet. How did you get my number?" Dre didn't see Ebony standing in the doorway. His answers were not only potentially detrimental to his freedom, but their future as well.

"You know that broad you used to fuck with. Wha—what was her name?" he asked. "Oh yeah, Monica. That's it!"

Dre slammed the phone down and turned around to see Ebony leaving out the doorway, satisfied with him standing on his promise to her.

EPILOGUE

It was summertime and the weather was almost as beautiful as the women were. The double wedding ceremony was held outside, in the backyard of Tony and Dee Dee's beautiful new colonial-style home. It was exactly a year to the date of Dre's welcome home party, as well as the night Tony and Dee Dee met. Smiles, laughter and tears of joy were everywhere; there was not a hint of the tragedies of the past year. It was a festive time, and everyone was with the person they wanted to be their world.

Dre and Tony stood at attention as they watched Ebony and Dee Dee walk down the aisle toward them. As the brides turned their backs to throw the bouquets, everyone gathered around. One fell into the hands of a

guest then laughter erupted when the other bouquet fell into E's hand.

"You know what that means, partna!" Dre hollered as he walked over to him. "I guess you're next." He patted Eric on the back.

Trina stood beside Eric, looking into his eyes. She hoped that he would ask her to marry him one day soon. Having witnessed the love, respect and devotion that Dee Dee and Ebony had for their men, she came to understand the meaning of loyalty. And, at that very moment, she was envious of them and wanted to know the love they experienced.

All of the formalities were over and the reception was about to start jumping off. All the fellas were on the dance floor stepping, each trying to prove that he had the most skills. The floor was filled with hundred dollar bills, to go to the best stepper. At that moment their women were the furthest things from their minds.

Ebony stopped the music and the girls went to claim their men, who always seemed to be huddled in a corner off to themselves whenever they got together. But, that was the bond they shared.

Before Dre and Ebony left for their honeymoon, Dre needed to make a stop. At the gravesite, he sat and talked to his mother and father for a while. It had been a long time since he last visited them and wanted them to know of the man that he had become. There were many

trials and tribulations, but he felt like he had it all together. The path of destruction that he was on seemed so obvious now, and he was surprised that he'd not seen it sooner.

From there, he stopped and paid his respects to his partna, Mookie. He felt responsible for his death and wished his partna could be there to share in some of the wealth that he acquired. Since he wasn't, Dre looked out for his family.

As he turned to leave, he was pulled in the direction where Monica lay, resting in peace, he hoped. He didn't know the right words to say. He just knew that it didn't have to turn out the way it did. Yet, he didn't blame himself, Tony or even her. Touching her tombstone as he walked away, he blamed the game and the chances that came with it. As he considered the deaths of Mookie, Monica, and even Rich, as well as the lives of J-Boogie, Dollar and Killa, he became overjoyed that he had raised and waved the white flag, and he never felt like less than a man for doing so.